Dear Minister,

Letters from a Public Servant

Amber Guette

A catalogue record of this book is available from the National Library of New Zealand.

ISBN 978-0-473-64588-5 (softcover)

ISBN 978-0-473-64589-2 (softcover POD)

ISBN 978-0-473-64590-8 (eBook)

Cover design by Melville Design

Layout by DIY Publishing Ltd

Amber Guette
Publishing Ltd

For Ruby and Liam — my most important contributions
to the public service and a better world

Contents

Preface

"The best way to find yourself is to lose yourself in the service of others" —*Mahatma Gandhi*

Why does good public service matter? In the words of an OECD report, "Government competence encompasses the ability to deliver quality public services, to respond to citizen needs and to effectively manage social, economic and political uncertainty." Trust is defined by the OECD as "a person's belief that another person or institution will act consistently with their expectations of positive behaviour". Every aspect of daily life in a democracy improves when public servants carry out their roles with integrity and competence.

These letters are the result of researching and following public servants' experiences under Westminster government systems for more than ten years to better understand what it means to be a public servant.

The fictitious country that this book is set in, 'Hooseland', (pronounced who's land) is a large developed western nation with a population of 42 million. The names of government departments and processes are generic, but recognisable by public servants working in these environments. The letters are the end result of real experiences and stories I have been told or read over that time.

It is likely that on reading these letters, no matter where you live, you will think you recognise individuals. That is because if I have learned one thing since I started my research it is that we share *many* issues and characteristics across our public service systems. There are people like the characters in these letters everywhere in our public service (or indeed any large organisation). Public servants that have read these letters have claimed they *definitely knew* who certain characters were, but every time they were wrong.

No character is based on any one person, but rather is a hybrid of multiple characteristics that fit that type of personality. This is the outcome I wanted – recognisable, but not identifiable. The goal is not to name and shame, but to shine a light on behaviour, good and bad, and to offer public servants the knowledge that they are not alone in their experiences. So, everything you will read here has happened at some point somewhere in our wider public service – this is not pure fiction, but rather 'faction' or fictionalised facts. Public service matters and our stories matter – that is the basis of these letters.

Blackbird

"They win by making you think you're alone"
Zorri Bliss, Star Wars: The Rise of Skywalker

Dear Reader

Now that the house of cards has fallen here in Hooseland I am going to share with you the letters I sent to Ministers over the last eight years. What started out as a once-a-month report from the frontlines to a Minister, hoping (in retrospect naively) that *if* they knew the truth things might improve for public servants, turned out to be the biggest battle of my life. These are the letters from the first four of those eight years, I am trying to recover the letters from the last four from a locked cloud platform after my laptop was stolen in a sting operation. I will share these for all the world to see in due course.

Time and hard experience have taught me that the public service is not just a place, it is also a concept. As servants of the public, we all have moral agency and the ability to make our own choices as to how we respond to things that happen.

Once upon a time the role of the public servant was a more sheltered one in Hooseland, for the most part kept away from the public eye, and our Ministers took responsibility for their Government's successes and failures. Those days have ended, and in the face of an increasingly 'politicised' public service I decided that it was time the tables were turned, and the political masters were 'publicservantised' so to speak.

Of course, as a public servant that was going to be a

bit tricky as most of us don't have any actual face to face contact with Ministers, only the well behaved and important ones get to do that. But I was growing weary of the 'water cooler' conversations and corridor grumblings about what was wrong in our world of work.

In my opinion Hooseland's public servants need to believe that real democracy and effective government are not just pipe dreams, but *essential to* the future of Hooseland. I do not believe either traditional left-wing or right-wing politics governments are the answer to the problems facing us and our planet. There is a strong need for practical and non-ideological solutions that provide an environment in which all people can reach their potential.

With that in mind, who is best placed to support humanity as we face the realities of successive governments failures to address issues such as climate change, food insecurity, growing threats to water supply, housing shortages, pandemics and other threats to our existence? Public servants. But – and this is a big but – we have much work to do to get our own house in order before we can truly become the ethical public service that listens respectfully to our public and demands higher standards of behaviour from our leaders and colleagues.

You see I am very proud of being a public servant and an important part of our mandate as public servants is to try to ensure the long-term good of the public. Yes, it is our role to ensure that our political masters policies are brought to life, but it is also our job to provide evidence-based policy advice on how to do that. They, of course, as elected representatives have the final decision on what happens, but in order for us to fulfil our mandate with integrity they should not be allowed to do so in wilful blindness to the consequences of those decisions.

In a world where climate change deniers are not just the lunatic fringe sitting alongside the 'flat earthers' and deep state alarmists, world leaders have the power to accelerate or slow down the pace at which the human race auto-genocides, and evidence-based policy is more essential than ever. Even in the worst-case scenario we will still need our public servants to act as the providers of palliative care to our species as we enter the final act.

But it is an imperfect world that we live in of course because humans are involved (tricky things humans). Some of you might say if you care that much about public service why are you exposing our foibles? Simple, for the same reasons a true patriot will criticise their country – because they believe it can and should be better. Nothing like a bit of sunlight to start a conversation on how we can be better.

If you are reading this and you are a public servant that understands what that means then you are my tribe, my chosen people. We have been dining on junk values in the Hooseland Public Service for too long. Just as junk food rots the body so junk values rot the soul – you cannot buy your way out of a soulless job – junk values mean our needs as human beings are not being met – we live in a machine designed to make us forget what is important about life and keep us being good little widgets. Well, for this public servant it was enough!

I decided to go straight to the source and find an amenable Minister that I could write to in a free and frank manner, without fear or favour, about once a month. As luck would have it, we had just had a change of government, so I decided to start writing before they lost that rosy glow of the newly engaged. This book is the sum of that correspondence. While the title of this book is *Dear Minister*, it is also a (tough) love letter to those of us that chose to serve the public – the lucky public servants.

Along the way while telling some of our stories (the good, the bad and the ugly), in retrospect when I decided to publish these letters, I thought they may also provide some public service 'hacks'. At its heart this collection of letters hoped to provide at least one Minister with a better understanding of why keeping the long-term good of the public at the heart of public service is so vital.

If you are not a public servant, then no doubt you know someone who is (I include nurses and teachers working in the public system in my widest definition). I wanted these letters to give voice to those who work or have worked in the service of the public and struggled with the behaviour of those around them. The aim was to talk truth to power, and I imagine there will be much that most public servants will recognise.

In our work we are called various things, depending on who is speaking. Civil servants, bureaucrats (I hate this one, but sadly some of us deserve to be called that at times) government servant, public official, pencil pusher, public servant, functionary... "the Deep State" (the paranoia behind this one literally has me on the floor laughing – if only they knew! Seriously, for those of you who are worried, no public service in the world is organised enough to pull that off – everyone who works in it knows the public service could never manage the kind of 'un-siloed' cooperation that would require!

Anyway, while I use the term public servant this should really be reserved for those that truly act in service and see this as a vocation, not just a job.

These letters celebrate those public servants that go the extra mile, work to understand the context and big picture of their work, serve with empathy, humour and treat people with dignity and take pride in what it means to be a public (not just government — we will leave that to the political advisers in their growing numbers) servant. They also delve into the not-so-great behaviour, because if we do not shine a light on that nothing will ever change.

So, what do I think public servants should aspire to? Simple — protecting the public good. At our best the guiding principle should be that we are not simply professionals, in it for our own gain, but for the public good above all else. Yes, sadly there are people working alongside us who, on balance, value their careers, their own personal gain or approval from their political masters above the public good. We have all worked with them from time to time.

They are still good people in their own way and sometimes contribute much to progressing things, but you can see the fear in their eyes if you talk too much about change or improving things or complain about political interference in operational work. They squirm and shuffle in their seats, exclude you from meetings, and call you a maverick — but more about them later.

To the ones that go out of their way every day to improve their service to the public, by creating efficiencies for hard working citizens tax dollars, or showing empathy and understanding to members of the public, through to the full-blown whistleblowers, taking massive personal risks in refusing to turn a blind eye to corruption and abuses of power — you are all heroes in my eyes.

And for the ones that have left after having been abused and broken by the system, I weep. Please come back — Hooseland needs you. I know, so much lip service is paid to the idea that we 'learn more from our mistakes than our successes' in the public service, because lord help you if you make one and find yourself 'thrown under the bus'. Come back with your experience and a new fire in your belly to be part of the renewal and re-purposing of the Hooseland Public Service in actual service of the public.

For those of you who have not seen the side of the Hooseland Public Service revealed in these letters I say mazeltov, you are blessed and long may it continue. For you this book may seem depressing at times, as ignorance is a sort of bliss, and because now the scales will have fallen from your eyes. But at least now you will know what you are seeing when you see it, and know to question it, and hopefully have some tools to deal with it. If not for your sake, then for the sake of your colleagues.

If you are a Higher-up or Top of the Totem Pole (TOTP) in a position to fight for what is right in the Hooseland Public Service, then think about what side of history you want to be on and choose wisely when you come to a crossroads.

And finally, for those that have seen corruption, but were too scared to do anything about it, I hear you, I see you. But I know that we are stronger together, and that the good we bring can far outweigh the bad that the selfish and powerful bring. It's reasonable to ask why I'm doing this. It boils down to a belief that honesty is an expression of loyalty in a healthy relationship, and I want a healthy public service for the citizens of Hooseland. We as public servants deserve better; the public deserves better. If you still think I may have exaggerated what I have reported, ask any public servant you know if the stories in these letters ring true. They say sunlight is the best disinfectant, and it is time to clean house.

Yours in service to the public,

Amber Guette

Amber Guette (she/her)

Everybody Wants to Rule the World

Dear Minister

Congratulations on winning a seat in the election! I have followed your rise with interest, and you seem to be as passionate about your work as I am about mine. Welcome to the public service. I hope your first month as a Minister for Hooseland is going well, you looked so chuffed yesterday when I saw you carrying your box of belongings into Parliament. You had that lovely glow of excitement when you were being sworn in (our team watched you on the midday news as you are our new Minister and our Higher-up even bought in a cake for the occasion).

By way of introduction, my name is Amber Guette, and I too am a public servant. This may be the first letter you have received directly from a public servant. I have a sneaking suspicion this is frowned upon, if not outright forbidden, but I did look at the Hooseland Public Service Code of Conduct, and there was nothing in there expressly forbidding it, so here goes. Unless you tell me to stop, it won't be the last time you hear from me.

You see I have been thinking about how to fix our public service here in Hooseland. I have seen too many issues being swept under the carpet and we need to change that for the sake of our public. I rather hope that if you know what's happening you can help with that change. In return, you may benefit from free and frank feedback from the frontlines.

Over the coming months, I want to share an insider's view of what it is like in our public service. You know – to look at what we do well, what we can do better, and what we just need to stop doing. A bit about my background may help explain why I am doing this and (potentially) risking my career as a public servant in Hooseland.

So, my mum was Irish and dad French. They both died way too soon in their 50's in a car accident, but they left me with a name (their idea of a joke) that I never get to forget while working in the public service – Amber Guette. Mum was a passionate Hooseland public servant and union representative, and dad was a journalist, they met when he was in the press gallery at parliament, and she was working in a Minister's office. And then I came along. Mum said she chose Amber because of its transparent qualities, and gave me the middle name Eslanda, which means 'truth' in Gaelic. My surname Guette translates from French into English as 'watchtower', so perhaps being the 'transparent truth watchtower' doomed me to take on the task of finding a way to communicate how things look from the frontlines. Either way, I believe they would approve of this minor act of rebellion.

I am just one of the many public servants whose job it is to help make your election promises come true. So, despite not voting for you, (yes, us public servants have political ideals same as everyone else, we just have to be careful how we express them), I was excited when your lot got elected, it felt like time for a change of government.

Our country needs some fresh thinking and bit of a shake up, and with spring upon us I am feeling full of optimism and hope. You come across as one of the more progressive ones, given the middle of the road choices we get these days (diversity is not just something the public service needs to work at harder you know).

On a personal level, I have done my homework and spoken with people that have worked alongside you. They generally say you have integrity and curiosity, that you genuinely care about outcomes, not just promotion to Cabinet or point scoring, so I hope that means you will allow me to continue. Of course, if you leave the red flag up on your letterbox at night on the first Tuesday of the month, I will take that as a sign you want me to stop, and I will end my missives.

Why am I taking the risk and doing this? To be honest, I am completely over the depressing, circular conversations with colleagues, the agreeing in hushed voices that something is wrong and needs to be fixed, the water-cooler conversations where people complain about things that usually end in some pragmatist saying, "well, we all know it's wrong, but that's just the way it is – so get used to it, it will catch up with them one way or another...". But it doesn't. There are no consequences. If anything, they get rewarded!

We watch them as they move quickly through the ranks (thanks to their finessed art of managing up and others promoting them to get them out of their departments) and become powerful and influential in the public service. That is how behaviour becomes institutionalised. So enough of the 'que sera sera' attitude. It may be naive of me to think that this could make a difference, but I must at least try.

I intend to write to you monthly about the things I think you need to know about our public service. Please bear with me – I am bound to go off-piste, or even lose my cool from time to time, I am passionate about this stuff and do not apologise for that.

If I am going to do this then it needs to be the plain honest truth, you of course, are free to ignore anything I say. At least I can then sleep better knowing I tried.

Apologies for delivering these to your home address (I got it from an ex-employee of yours who also thinks you deserve to know the truth), it likely feels a *wee* bit stalkerish, but we both know that if I go through the formal channels, you will never see them, and the letters would just become an in-joke amongst your private secretaries and political adviser's. Or more likely, be used as a witch hunt by my risk averse Manager to silence me. I don't want or expect a response and will happily take your silence as permission to continue.

This isn't a case of airing dirty laundry – it is meant with love for our public and my colleagues and comes from a strong belief that we can and must do better as public servants. The public interest test demands that it is time to put the ideal of 'free and frank' advice fully into practice. I want to find a way to make things better for those we jointly serve – the public.

As I said – you are our new Minister, as I also happen to work for one of your portfolio government departments – Community Health Advisory Operations & Services *(CHAOS)*, however, that is not the sole focus of what I am writing to you about. I have worked in many different departments and have followed the trials and tribulations of Westminster system public servants globally for many years out of curiosity (we all need hobbies...) and have learnt that there is more in common in our experiences than people would think.

Many of my colleagues think the faults in the system have been there so long that things will never change. I refuse to accept that, even though I do feel like our world has gone a bit mad. I read Orwell's *1984* and Atwood's *The Handmaids Tale* as a teenager and the older I get the more I see them as prophetic warnings of things to come if we do not keep checks and balances on power.

The long-term best interest of the public demands our considered thinking and a strategic approach to implementation of the new policies your Government will bring to the table, not blind obedience.

So, let's begin and I will try my best to explain what it is like on our side of the bargain and how things might improve.

P.S. I hope you will take the time to listen to the song recommendations in the title of the letters I will send – they are not *essential* to the letters but may help get across the zeitgeist of them.

Yours in service to the public,

Amber Guette

Amber Guette (she/her)

Learning To Fly

Dear Minister

Your second month in as a new Minister! I guess the reality of being a Minister and the workload that brings is starting to sink in.

I was very pleased to drive past and not see the red flag up on your letterbox last night. Thank you for giving me this opportunity to share our world with you. Time to let you in on what it is like to be a public servant. At its heart working in the public service is like being part of a family. A large, diverse, dysfunctional family with plenty of wise grandparents, sibling rivalry, amusing cousins and weird uncles...

One of the most common things I hear people say at their leaving morning teas is that it is the people that make it a good place to work. And they are right, the majority of people I have worked with have been amazing. Most of us can say hand on heart that we are here most of the time to make a difference for Hooselanders. But it should be all of us, all of the time, thinking as we go about our work, does this make a difference? Does this make the lives of Hooselanders better?

So yes, while the best of the best people you could possibly hope to work with are working in our public service, so unfortunately, are some of the worst. I often think about how we are portrayed in the media or on TV etc, and such historical treasures such as *Yes Minister* come to mind, or more recently, *In the Thick of It*, personally I can't get enough of Malcolm Tucker, the old sweary fairy!

But if you really want to understand our day-to-day reality, I don't think you can go past the Australians take on public service in *Utopia*. They have a particularly laconic and accurate sense of humour when it comes to the public service, watching *Utopia* I never know whether to laugh or cry. The daily frustrations the head of the fictitious, National Building Authority Tony and his colleague Nat face ring far too true for so many of us in the public service, Rob Sitch deserves a knighthood for services to the public for portraying our environment in such an accurate way. Totally worth a watch if you want a crash course on 'Public Service 101'.

On a good day we go to work knowing that we have a chance to make a material difference to the lives of thousands of people. There are still those of us that see this as a vocation and not just a paycheck or career move. It is an opportunity to provide service to the public with honesty, respect, fairness and compassion. That is if we can successfully avoid the blockers, the bullies, and at times, crippling risk averseness and bureaucracy. Sometimes, given the right environment, we may even be able to approach our work with zest, and truly reach our potential. But for that to happen on the regular we need to work together to create the public service that the public and public servants deserve.

Okay, so to do this, I think we need to change the way we view public service. The traditional role of government as paternalistic problem solver is way past its use by date. We need to cultivate a collaborative problem solving culture. One that will enable us to work with the public, civil society organisations and the private sector to address the massive (future and current) challenges we face as a planet. That is surely where our greatest value lies? As the coordinators, bridge builders, stewards, facilitators, the midwives, and sadly at this rate, the palliative care providers, for the planet?

Right now, our public service is not typically seen as an optimistic workplace. It is a bit of a lottery, and if you get the wrong ticket, you will be faced with an unending parade of restructures, incompetent managers and in some departments, an overall toxic culture. For the less fortunate, the Higher-ups (a blanket term for all middle managers in the Hooseland Public Service) hold power over them, not only as direct supervisors but as the gatekeepers of their future employment.

Some public servants can find themselves locked into their jobs, dependent on their Higher-up for a reference, and if that Higher-up has it in for them, their lives will be miserable. You can imagine what that means for the quality of experience they will bring to the public.

In some environments, being a professional and being passionate about your job is actually viewed with suspicion, as certain old school leaders believe the public service profession should be 'dispassionate'. But this can lead to two-dimensional public servants who fail to grasp the complex messiness and intricacies of public service life (which just reflects the realities of the lives of the public they serve). Nothing is black and white.

I have watched public servants that just did what they are told and never questioned if it was the best way of doing things. They do not take initiative, or show independent thought, and they *never* take it upon themselves to do anything that has not been rubber stamped by the Higher-ups.

The sad thing is that the people who have the values that the public service says it wants can't work in that kind of system. If you care and take it to heart when you see these things happening, you can get very disillusioned. I have watched colleagues start out as enthusiastic, positive caring people and walk away completely burnt out and cynical with their time in the Hooseland Public Service. Higher-ups and TOTPs need to *trust* public servants to get on with the work at hand, and not kill their initiative by micromanaging.

Fear plays a big part in these environments; people go into meetings too scared to speak for fear of saying the wrong thing. One of my colleagues told me about one such Higher-up, apparently, they had been told by her that they weren't allowed to speak in her meetings. And she wouldn't even acknowledge them in the corridor. She was known for coming into a room and only acknowledging certain people that were in her good books, and not acknowledging the others.

How do these people get promoted? We often scratch our heads and wonder that out-loud with each other. This fear is well placed − one of the most terrifying things I have seen in the Hooseland Public Service is how Higher-ups (and *their* Higher-up's − the TOTP's) can destroy a public servant's career − their livelihood, their mental health and their family's well-being. This extreme form of bullying is an insidious form of corruption as it is used to keep us quiet, and to allow the perpetrator to go unchecked.

As you can probably tell, integrity matters to me − a lot. Like more than just about anything and especially when it comes to the public service. I am not religious or engaged in many hobbies other than trying to understand the public service, so let's just say public service integrity is my religion/hobby. I was so excited when I entered the Hooseland Public Service, I joined because I wanted a seat at the table so I could help improve things for the public.

That was before my Emperor's New Clothes moment, when I realised, I needed to be making a difference for my fellow public servants, not just the public.

So, this month's song 'learning to fly' is about my rather (naive in retrospect) high hopes in joining the public service, 'coming down is the hardest thing'. Yes, yes, it is. I had so many questions and no books that I could find to give me the answers. I stumbled around at the start asking questions like, "but surely you have a process for that?", "But why do we do that – that can't be the best use of resources?", "Is that seriously okay for them to talk to us that way?" And sometimes in the face of serious bullshit – "why is no one saying anything!?", "Why would someone behave that way?", "Don't we have a code of conduct!?", you get the picture.

I don't imagine entering politics was much different for you, full of dreams about how you were going to change the world, fix the inequities, make the system better, stronger, more responsive and less wasteful of resources, etc. So how do you learn to fly when you ain't got wings. Simple – you wing it. You learn, as my Canadian friend Nick Charney would say, to *"scheme virtuously"*. You watch, you listen, you learn. You pick your battles, and you work to change things by stealth, by conversations, leading by doing, sticking up for people and yourself. By promoting all things positive.

Clearly focusing on negatives at work was not going to get me anywhere, so my wings were built by promoting the good bits I saw everywhere I went in the public service. If there was a code of conduct and I felt someone was breaching it, I tried to find a way to point that out without making people angry.

I was raised to treat everyone with the same amount of respect irrespective of who they are – CEO or cafeteria staff

— until they actively lose that respect. So, in my ideal public service when we see something good being done — tell people, or if you see a colleague struggling — support them.

We are all human, we have our failings, but if at the heart of it we have the service of others at the core of what we do then we can make a difference. I am sure we both have examples of good and even great things happening in our realms, where people really made a difference because they stood up for what was right in the face of opposition.

This kind of environment has major implications for how the public service behaves and interacts with the public. Surely our role as public servants is to act as guardians of what belongs to the public, to serve and safeguard their interests? On that note it would be great if your side of the equation could remember that ultimately you are public servants as well.

We see too much of Ministers behaving like they have Stockholm Syndrome, constantly looking over their shoulder to see what the Opposition will say, who do you serve? Them or the public that voted you in? Be bold, do the right thing, you have been chosen by the people of Hooseland to lead!

The bottom line for both of our workplaces is that public accountability means including the public — and listening, understanding and responding to them.

Yours in service to the public,

Amber Guette

Amber Guette (she/her)

Under Pressure

Dear Minister

Spring is fully flung, and I hope you are making the most of it. Have you watched Utopia yet? Seriously, it is the best example I can give you of what working in the public service looks like. I am *very* excited to be working on your new state-of-the-art community health care clinics project, not *so* excited about the whole 'first one hundred days' bit — but we will do our best to get this up and running as fast as we possibly can, while trying to ensure it is robust, and meets the CHAOS quality criteria....

So, this month I want to tell you about the pressures we can face as public servants, pressure from your end (those first 100 days plans are great for getting momentum going, but not *always* a good way to get the best and most accurate advice out of the public service), pressure from the public, pressure from the Opposition, the media, pressure from stressed out bosses, etc. I know you understand as your job must see you in some intensely pressured situations at times.

On a more positive note, we know you want to make your mark, hit the ground running and all, but perhaps it is sometimes better to under promise and over deliver rather than vice-versa? Just a thought....

It is exciting having a new Government, but you need to get used to us and we need to get used to you, show you what's under the table so to speak, where the bodies are buried and ensure that all the exciting things you promised in opposition are doable and in what timeframes, always with an eye to what is in the best interest of the public.

Don't get me wrong, no one is more excited than me to see a government that understands spending on social services is crucial to our success as a democracy and to give the next generation a fighting chance, but perhaps getting it done right is more important than getting it done fast? And believe me we do know how to do fast when it is needed.

I wish you could see us when we get an oral parliamentary question and the clock starts ticking... full blown crazy – a war room of public servants doing their very best to get answers to the question, background material, dream up possible supplementary questions and answers, statistics and graphs to back up the questions and answers, fact-checkers making sure we have it correct, others searching previous answers to written parliamentary questions, media articles and wracking our brains to try and fathom what could possibly be going on in the mind of the feckless Opposition member that asked it, and whether anything could have been leaked to them. And that is just an ordinary run of the mill question.

When we get one like we did this week the pressure shoots off the register. You see we are here to serve you – and also to be transparent and answer the public and the media's questions via the 'Act' (not the one that goes on in the Speaker's chair as a rite of passage for nearly every drunken staffer at parliament), I am referring to "The Act" – the Access to Publicly Funded Information Act (APFIA).

As public servants we have our day-to-day workload, which in the exciting age of doing more with less, is normally more than enough to earn our keep. And we accept that we will have extra work that comes hurtling at us out of the blue (often because someone else has not done their bit in a timely manner) and is deemed URGENT!

In our world 'urgent' does not ring any alarm bells as it gets used rather flippantly. Any 'urgent' piece of work will usually quickly be followed up by something even more 'urgent'. It can start to get to the hysterical stage (the unhinged kind, not the good funny kind) at times, with competing levels of "well is it just urgent? Or urgent, urgent? or urgent, urgent, urgent??" On bad days these are real measures we use to decide how to prioritise our work.

We get it, sometimes things are *genuinely* urgent. Like for instance, when you are in the House being grilled by the Opposition at Question Time and need a response yesterday. In those situations, you will find us running like the wind and using telepathy amongst other ninja skills to save you from embarrassment, and to ensure democracy is best served with the correct response. We are here to serve and take that role seriously. Please use this power wisely.

Short-term bursts of adrenaline are fine, they keep up our fight or flight reflexes, and no one *seriously* minds having lunch at 4 pm every now and then. However, you should bear in mind that *some* people in your office like to use your power to make requests with very short turnaround timeframes, in order to give themselves the luxury of a week to look at it before adding their partisan feedback to it. Add to that, nothing can leave the building without about six levels of approval from assorted Higher-ups (spreads the blame if something goes wrong, I think?) and you start to get the picture. And that is when the department is functioning. But more on ensuring smooth sailing between political advisers and public servants later.

I know this picture of frenetic public servants sits at odds with the stereotype of government as slow-moving. But the truth is these days public servants are working very hard with shrinking resources, lack of office space, growing demand from the public and Ministers, and impossibly outdated technology (in my previous job I had a 2006 laptop, with lotus notes and IBM?? What is this, the dark ages?). Add to all this the non-stop 'urgent' information requests. This can create a relentlessly operational workplace, where the urgent crowds out the important, with little time for the luxury of learning and reflection and creating insightful, long-term interventions for the public.

Of course, it is not just the workload, but the culture in which you have to work that can add to the pressure. A colleague told me about a certain tier two, or Top of the Totem Pole (TOTP – the term TOTP covers all tier one and two managers in Hooseland Public Service speak), nicknamed 'Cruella', that made their life so difficult it was like being in an abusive relationship. Coming into work each day like some beaten wife waiting to see what mood Cruella was in. That is very clearly not right, no one needs that extra pressure in a job that is already well stocked with a range of pressures and deadlines, certainly no one needs moody, self-indulgent and destructive behaviour from their work colleagues and Higher-ups.

Our younger, more timid or less experienced public servants often do not know what to say when leapt upon with the fourth *very* urgent request of the day, often in the face of multiple, other competing priorities. Given the nature of most departments work it is *highly* unlikely anyone is going to die if something gets done the next day.

My advice to public servants (or perhaps even new Ministers?) who are being put through the wringer on a daily basis, is to keep a running list of their work and when faced with such requests say "of course, happy to help" and then put on their best and most helpful face and showing them the list ask their Higher-up if they would like to help them re-prioritise the rest of their work so that they can ensure they are getting them done in the correct order? This is a much better tactic than just saying sod off, having a meltdown, or burning out and leaving the job.

I often see the 'Keep Calm and Carry-On' meme in public service, and to be honest, keeping calm is probably the best thing to try and do in these situations, rather than getting stressed out over something that you either a) have no control over or b) was a totally unreasonable request to begin with. I am not always naturally a calm person as you may have guessed, but I admire those that are. The best thing we can have is a Higher-up that sets boundaries with both the staff in a Ministers' office and in ours. For the system to change, our participants need to change the way they behave.

The cult of too much pressure also detracts from our department's vision, firstly because people are too busy sweating the small stuff, worrying about covering the urgent work at the expense of their day job, (which is hopefully one where they feel they can make progress), while Higher-ups are too busy focusing on maintaining control and approving the constant flow of requests. All the while, neither is focused on the end goal of working towards a culture of collective progress.

When our work purpose matches our personal purpose, public servants are energised, which leads to greater engagement levels, higher motivation, productivity, critical thinking, a solutions mindset, healthy debate, teamwork, creativity, agility and, ultimately, a strong work culture.

The question remains – are we building a government service cult or a public service culture?

Yours in service to the public,

Amber Guette

Amber Guette (she/her)

Canadian Please

Dear Minister

First day of summer! This month I wanted to let you in on some of the ways that Hooseland public servants have tried to improve our lot within our workplaces. I don't want you thinking I have come to you to solve all our problems, we are quite capable of doing that ourselves given the right environment – and of course, support from the right people in government ;-).

Allow me to explain further to you the concept of 'scheming virtuously', or more precisely *Scheming Virtuously for Public Servants* (although I am sure plenty of this is also applicable in your world).

About ten years ago a small group of us got excited about wanting to help fellow public servants deal with some of the obstacles and pressures we face, so we did some hunting around on the Internet to find similar minded people. There was very little out there that wasn't highly academic and of little use in the frontlines (we needed to hear our own voices not those of external commentators!).

Finally, we discovered some clever Canadian public servants who had started the Canadian Public Sector Renewal organisation (we *definitely* need a Hooseland Public Sector Renewal organisation). Grassroots public servants doing it for themselves – just what we were looking for! The most impressive, and useful resource for me at the time (2014) was a very cool booklet called – Scheming Virtuously for Public Servants. This is not a "what–to-do" manual, it's a "how-to" manual (personally I think of it as the public servant's bible).

The first thing that caught my eye was a statement at the start they had quoted from the 2008 Report of the Clerk on the Public Service of Canada: "Renewal is not about fixing something for all time but updating what we do and how we do it in order to remain relevant and effective now and into the future. It is about keeping the institution of the public service dynamic, fresh and respected. And renewal is not something others do; the impetus for renewal has to come from within, and it has to involve all of us." Hooray!

This is what *we* wanted to achieve, taking the words supplied by our Higher-ups – the mission statement for the public service and such like, and making it our own, taking back responsibility for and control of *our* working conditions. I contacted them and discovered that everything they had to say resonated with our thinking about how Hooseland Public Service renewal had to come from within. It is not some change of culture that could be imposed from outside by a 'Change Management' team (lord I have seen some truly *awful* work done by teams with this moniker), or even from the Higher-ups of the public service (of course for these things to really take off it does require 'tone at the top' that supports it, or it risks turning into a battle with management...).

From our Canadian comrades we heard that while the vast majority of public servants may not have direct input into how the public service addresses the challenges facing us at the macro-level, *all of us* have the ability to address the challenges where they are most important, at the micro-level. Public servants are connected by a common responsibility for the system as a whole.

They defined public service renewal more broadly than we

had seen the Higher-ups in Hooseland do, asserting that its primary concern is not "staffing up" or retaining employees, but "cultivating a culture of stewardship and innovation". Sigh... music to our ears – thank you Canada!

The key to all of this, they noted, is to not let your imagination and enthusiasm be dampened by organisational politics or institutional caution (easier said than done at times). Instead, you need to "be deliberate: look for weaknesses in your organisation's existing practises, maximise your advantage and create new opportunities to argue for change." Oh wow! We had hit the jackpot. But sadly, life and work got in the way, and once we found that the Higher-ups did not want anything to do with our grassroots efforts, our band of merry public servants went off in other directions in search of the holy grail of better public service.

Nearly a decade later I found a copy of it in my archives last week and dusted it off, made copies and provided it to some of my colleagues – I watched their eyes sparkle and from their comments I could confirm it had not aged at all, it was still as relevant and fresh as ever. It is full of sage advice, and not just for those new to the public service either, like the following gems:

- Before scheming, explicitly identify your discussion as a safe space. Allaying the concerns of participants before the discussion starts will ease the flow of information. So too will sharing a personal story of your own experience with the issue. Building trust is the key to scheming safely. Trust has to be earned, and it tends to be earned slowly. But once trust is established you can really dig into the issues at hand.
- Want fresh eyes? There is no better way to get a frank and honest question or opinion than to ask a new hire. Who cares if they have no experience with the question? New

arrivals are likely to give you a gut reaction and more importantly, one that isn't filtered through govspeak.

- Focus on the opportunities, not the problems. Don't let the discourse be dominated by the people afflicted by "this will never work because" disease. Focus on why your idea is a good one.

- At the end of the day, you need to be able to look yourself in the mirror and feel proud of what you have accomplished and what is yet to come, and if that means bending the rules to achieve the results you believe in, then so be it as long as you are willing to own it, for better or for worse.

I love these guys! Sometimes I think that maybe it is time to get the old gang back together to work on renewal? But the reality is that the culture has not changed in the Hooseland Public Service leadership, and until it does, I guess we will be faced with the same challenges we had before. We put our heads up above the parapet back then and met with some of the Higher-ups, but our offers back then of sharing feedback from our grassroots membership on ways to improve the public service were met with stony faces then, and no doubt would be again.

Perhaps if we can somehow get the TOTPs to buy in we really could fix things? I know one thing for certain, the political game playing, bullying, blocking and generally rubbish behaviour of way too many Higher-ups has to change *somehow*. Even if it were sustainable (which it isn't) it is just so toxic there is no way we can meet our obligations as servants of the public under these conditions, no way we can live our best lives as public servants, citizens and family members.

Please, Minister, help us fix this? I will leave you with my favourite quote from *Scheming Virtuously for Public Servants*:

"Don't be a Dead Hero – This should go without saying, but whatever you do – don't be an idiot. You are no good to your organisation as a dead hero. Sure, you raised a stink about whatever, people cheered (in their heads), but in the end you have accomplished nothing because no one in their right mind is willing to collaborate or champion something that was just over-advocated by someone who stirred the pot with reckless disregard.

Remember that your relationships and reputation are your best assets, and that your actions impact both of these assets considerably. They also impact those around you so take care in managing them.

At its core, scheming virtuously is about using your judgement to make decisions that you can live with while creating a culture of innovation and stewardship within the public service."

Yours in service to the public,

Amber Guette

Amber Guette (she/her)

Truth and Freedom

Dear Minister

I hope you are enjoying the latest news cycle with what looks like a new conspiracy theory about the Government popping up every second day. Given this is so topical it seems like a good time to talk about "Deep State" conspiracy theories. I feel like we could both do with a laugh.

Firstly, going back to first principles, anyone who has ever worked in government knows full well that the kind of organisation and cooperation that it would take to pull that kind of effort off is non-existent. We all know that government departments leak like sieves – and given internal rivalries, well... good luck to anyone trying to control the narrative in *that* environment. Never assign to malice what is explained by incompetence, or to quote Ben Franklin, three people can keep a secret if two of them are dead.

One of my favourite colleagues, Anthony from Finance, explained to me the other day that the people who believe in conspiracy theories are really just looking for simple answers to life's chaotic happenings (a bit like religion) they just want to know *someone* is responsible. The truth is more frightening, no one is in control! Jesus take the wheel... anyway, I look on them a little more kindly now that I know that.

So that brings me to what the Hooseland Public Service can do to help ensure that the public don't feel like we *are* hiding anything from them, because we surely do not help matters in the way that we deal with information. I gather you know all about how that works of course? They cover it in the Machinery of Government course provided to all new Ministers. I have heard the uptake is not great, but of course completing that course should be compulsory, like a warrant of fitness for Ministers. A rather embarrassing lack of knowledge as to how government works is possibly the single biggest pain in the neck for public servants working with new Ministers....

Back to the Act, I am getting rather tired of fighting to get people in your team and mine to understand that responding to requests under the Act is not a nuisance designed to keep them from their 'real work', but an extremely important part of the democratic process. I think a few of them could benefit from doing that Machinery of Government course too.... What they do not seem to understand is that the reason, and spirit, in which the Act was created, was to provide the public with full access to as *much* of the information generated by governments as possible.

The Acts' clauses on the grounds as to why some bits of information can be withheld or refused were put there to balance the need to release information with the public interest, and to protect the privacy of individuals.

Instead, over the years it seems to have become a perverse game of cat and mouse, whereby public servants are expected by the TOTP and Ministers' offices to make it as *difficult* as possible for the public to access information. Last week we had staff in your office fudging an answer to an APFIA on the basis that it requested details of the "code *of* compliance certificate" for one of the new clinics, when it was technically called a "code compliance certificate". Steve in our office is usually on the side of such dodgy behaviour, but even he said "Well that is a dick move..." It is *not* the role of government in a democracy to manipulate the flow of information, that is exactly the type of behaviour that creates the conditions for conspiracy theories to flourish in.

The 'no-surprises' approach to releasing official information should be just that – a heads up for your office that this information has been requested and that it is going into the public realm. Not as an opportunity for Ministers' staff to be given a week to make multiple changes to the departments proposed release.

One of the weirdest examples of this that I have witnessed was an APFIA that came into the CHAOS team. We looked at it and all agreed within five minutes that what was requested was not information held by CHAOS, and as far as we could tell information that did not exist at all in any other department. So quite clearly the answer was no – pretty simple right? Nope. Even though the answer was "we do not have this information", after it went through the multiple Higher-up sign outs, their risk averseness insured that it still had to go to the Ministers' office for review (!). Two weeks later they came back to us and said that because of *who* was asking, a 'no' was not an appropriate response. It was another month of back and forth before the poor requester got a very late, (the department had used every legal trick in the book to extend the timeframes...) very wordy, two-page response that at the end of the day said, "we do not have this information". They must have thought we were completely bonkers....

My other pet peeve is public servants who seem to have a fetish for stamping 'CONFIDENTIAL' on everything. I keep asking them to be a little more judicious before they watermark documents this way, as it is a major red flag for the requester when they get redacted documents with that on them. What might have looked like just more boring policy speak takes on a whole new life and level of scrutiny.

They keep telling me that they will be more careful, but I see no evidence of that yet. These clever clogs do the same with putting 'FREE & FRANK' as a subject line in their emails. I then have to break their hearts by explaining to them that putting that as a subject in an email, does *not* automatically make their correspondence immune to release, but it does make it much more exciting for a journalist or Opposition MP to get in their release bundle. It seems to be an automatic, knee-jerk, bureaucratic reaction to use these terms as magic talismans to keep prying eyes out simply because it has always been done before, and some public servants seem to have difficulty getting out of that habit.

Finally, I have had several APFIA responses drafted by our team come back from review by your office with whole chunks crossed out and the red pen comments such as "not asked for in their request". Do they think we are completely stupid? Of course, we know what was, and what was not asked for, but have they ever heard of being helpful? If you look objectively at what is left by the time they have done their deletions, it raises more questions for the requester than it does answer their genuine concerns!

Providing information that gives the requester a bit of context on the information being released, and a much more satisfying response, goes a long way to increasing their confidence that the government might actually know what it is doing. We are here to be helpful, not obstructive – the name of the game is on the tin so to speak – Access to Publicly Funded Information. They have paid for it with their hard-earned tax dollars and deserve transparency and respect from the government, not obfuscation and contempt.

Anyway, if you did manage to attend the Machinery of Government course, then I am certain you will have picked up on the guidance that Ministers should exercise a professional approach and good judgement in their interactions with public servants. It is *crucial* that Hooseland Ministers respect the political neutrality of the public service and not request that public servants act in a way that conflicts with the integrity of their roles as public servants.

While I have no doubt that you personally intend to act with the highest of integrity levels, it would be helpful if when you see your colleagues stepping over that invisible – but highly important – line that separates our worlds, that you remind them why it is there, to protect not just Ministers and public servants, but the Hooseland public as well.

Yours in service to the public,

Amber Guette

Amber Guette (she/her)

The Human Centipede

Dear Minister

In the course of my research into public service behaviour, I have learnt some new words (actually quite a *few* new words) this week, the number one new word being – bureaupathologies. These are rather quaintly described as the "vices, maladies and sickness of bureaucracies" very Victorian sounding language. I thought it might be fun to find out what exactly these bureaupathologies were, and provide a comprehensive list of them for you, so here goes!

Abuse of authority/power/position, Arbitrariness, Arrogance, Bias, Blurring issues, Boondoggles, Bribery, Bureaucratese (unintelligibility), Busywork, Carelessness, Chiselling, Coercion, Complacency, Compulsiveness, Conflicts of interest/objectives, Conspiracy, Corruption, Counter-productiveness, Cowardice, Criminality, Deadwood, Deceit, Dedication to status quo, Discourtesy, Discrimination, Dogmatism, Dramaturgy, Empire-building, Favouritism, Fear of change, Finagling, Foot-dragging, Gattopardismo (superficiality), Incompetence, Indecision (decidophobia), Indifference, Ineptitude, Inertia, Inflexibility, Inhumanity, Injustice, Insensitivity, Intimidation, Kleptocracy, Leadership vacuums, Malfeasance, Malice, Malignity, Managing-up, Mindlessness, Miscommunication, Misconduct, Misfeasance, Misinformation, Negativism, Negligence, Nepotism, Neuroticism, Obscurity, Obstruction, Officiousness, Oppression, Overkill, Paperasserie, Paranoia, Patronage, Perversity, Procrastination, Punitive supervision, Red-tape, Reluctance to delegate, Reluctance to take decisions, Sabotage, Self-perpetuation, Self-serving, Sloppiness, Social astigmatism, Soul-destroying work, Stagnation, Stalling, Stonewalling, Sycophancy, Territorialism, Tokenism, Tunnel vision, Unfairness, Unnecessary work, Unprofessional, Unreasonableness, Usurpation, Vanity, Vested interest, Vindictiveness, Waste, Xenophobia.

Whew – quite the list! These would make for a great game of Public Servant Behaviour Bingo to see how many of these behaviours we have witnessed over the years. I don't imagine they will let us do *that* as a team building exercise at our next away day....

Anyway, today I just want to focus on one of these bureaupathologies to start with – the practice of 'managing up'. Look I get it, every job has *some* level of managing up required, but when this becomes the *sole focus* and motivation of that person, it guarantees that they are not doing their job in serving the public.

Again, plenty of great people in the public service, so I cannot for the life of me understand why the Hooseland Public Service seems to favour promoting the ones that have built their careers by kissing up to those above them (or for that matter anyone else further up the hierarchy they think can help them get what they want) and kicking those below them (hmm... my old TOTP friend Cruella seems to spring to mind yet again...).

I imagine that you sometimes have similar problems in your party, so I am hoping you can relate to the topic of this week's letter. I refer, rather grandly, to this as my "Matryoshka Doll Theory of Public Management". This theory explains the Public Service practice of "managing up" and how it can get taken to rather unfortunate extremes in Hooseland.

To start on the right foot, I need to state that the art of managing up can be a real positive if it is done for the right reasons, say with a focus on ensuring that Higher-ups have an honest view of what is going on at the coalface. I have seen this done really well in the past by a Higher-up I once had. Time to introduce you to Susan H. I may at times seem pretty dark on Hooseland Higher-ups in my letters, but I have seen some excellent ones in my time, and Susan H is a good example of what great looks like (sadly, as we all know no good deed goes unpunished, but more on that later).

Susan H had the unenviable role of trying to ensure her new TOTP understood the nature of the issues facing CHAOS before they leapt in and made all kinds of uninformed, and frankly, bad decisions. I had already watched her navigate what I saw as blatant stonewalling from the existing TOTP prior to this new appointment, as she worked really hard with our team to achieve everything we needed to fulfil our work programme. She genuinely strived to support CHAOS in making a difference for the public.

She was passionate, intelligent, street smart, humorous, and had a great sense of justice. She didn't micromanage – in fact she seemed pretty happy with my 'ask for forgiveness not permission' approach to my role and was happy for us all to just get on with the job we were paid to do. She was not blind to the need to manage expectations of those above her, but unfortunately, they were so busy doing their own managing up, that the needs of our team never got beyond them to the top of the hierarchy. It is a bit like an extreme form of reverse constipation....

In the Matryoshka Doll scenarios information flows down, but feedback from the frontlines on the honest repercussions of the Higher-ups decisions often seems to stop at the first leader in the hierarchy. This explains why I call it the

"Matryoshka Doll theory of Public Management". They have their heads so far up the person in front of them that they cannot see what is happening for those below them. Or, even if they can, they see nothing to be gained by sharing that with the next level of the hierarchy.

Now, add to that, if you have an upward facing that never spends anytime talking to those at the front line, (I have even heard of TOTPs taking the stairs so as not to be stuck in the lift with an employee) and you have the perfect storm. Often these TOTP's see their role as managing the Minister, not leading their department, and in the worst cases yelling at all those below them that their role is to "just give the Minster what they want" no matter the consequences (and I have seen that backfire and have rather *negative* consequences for Ministers), and to keep the Minister and the department out of the media, unless of course, it is positive news.

This creates a toxic environment that becomes a swirl of risk averse arse covering and bullying, as the Higher-ups jockey for position to be keeping the TOTP happy and thus progressing their own careers. Also why *exactly* do we give public servant's knighthoods in Hooseland?? Surely, they are paid very well already to do their job by the public. Should we not be saving those accolades for the ones who do wonderful things that are otherwise unrecognised or rewarded?

What we really need is a public service where we can protect the people without power by having the ability to safely raise problems to those who have it. My letters will touch on these issues and the need for a way for public servants to not just "whistleblow" when things are really dodgy, but also to seek support in addressing toxic behaviour.

We both know that when there are no consequences for people's bad behaviour there are enormous repercussions for the workplace. For me this is about the cornerstone of good public service, integrity.

We need practical integrity systems that do not risk the careers of good public servants for calling out bad behaviour by their colleagues. I think that, coupled with an independent Public Service Ombudsman to deal with more serious allegations and whistleblowing, could go a long way to getting rid of many of the bureaupathologies listed (not exhaustively I might add) above.

Internal reporting in an environment that is the cause of the problem is pointless and will only put the person raising the issue at risk. A Code of Conduct in the public service is all very well, but only if it is *enforced* and not just empty words. Like everything this all starts at the top – we seriously need TOTPs that walk the talk. But more on that later.

Yours in service to the public,

Amber Guette

Amber Guette (she/her)

P.S. I could not find a song about Matryoshka Dolls, but I explained how it worked to Steve in IT, and he told me there was a movie called "The Human Centipede" that kind of summed it up, and he said luckily there *was* a song about that. I must watch it, Steve said it was his favourite movie ever.

Psycho Killer

Dear Minister

One of the conversation starters that always gets a good response in the public service is to ask people "have you ever worked with a psychopath or sociopath?" *Everyone* has a story to tell. We had one in a department I worked in, they seemed so pleasant to start with. It was quite jaw dropping how they behaved, but worse was the way that management dealt with them.

This particularly special person excelled at gas lighting people, including the Higher-ups they reported to, which would seem like a great way to get fired. They had a job to do, but never really seemed to *do it* – they would seriously do anything *but* their job, including inserting themselves in other people's work, trying to pass their colleagues work off as their own by changing two words in a document, and blatantly ignoring requests made by their Higher-up in such a way that their Higher-up started to think *they* were going mad because it just made no sense that someone would behave that way to a Higher-up.

But for the sociopath once they have decided that particular Higher-up is no longer of any use to them, they will fall victim to the same behaviour the rest of the team is suffering. This kind of behaviour doesn't happen quickly, as I said, it is more of a 'boiled frog syndrome'. They can start out charming as heck, but one day you realise that you need to save all your emails, and that if a certain someone has a penchant for making phone calls rather than emailing, you had better make sure that any decisions or advice followed is reflected back to them in an email if you do not want to be later in a position where you are blamed, or they totally misrepresent what was agreed, or what they said or told you to do, as you sit there incredulously wondering how this person is lying in such a bold faced way??

And all the while they will be ensuring that they are getting in good with the next opportunity – spending the time they should be just getting on with their work trying to impress some poor gullible Higher-up in another department and climbing ranks that way. And their current Higher-up – are they going to say anything? Not likely if it means they continue to be stuck with the problem.

One of the characteristics of these people is that they are often unpredictable. One minute calm, the next flying into a rage. This unpredictable and aggressive behaviour keeps the rest of us in a constant state of high anxiety. Everyone desperately hopes that they are not going to be the next target. This strategy is used by the psychopath to maintain control over people.

The organisation's culture is an importance influence on an individual's behaviour, especially when the threat of repercussions is minimal, or absent as it can be in the public service. These litigious public servants learn to keep their jobs not by their merit, but because they threaten weak Higher-ups with legal action if they called out on their behaviour.

They are a double disaster, as not only are they not doing their work, but often they will actively block work that urgently needs to happen. Refusing to provide information requested in an APFIA, joining in an email chain and then creating chaos by changing perfectly good responses just to make their mark. These individuals are so bad that often good people having to work with them eventually just leave in order to not have to deal with them ever again.

Higher-ups do not want personal grievance cases against them on their record (death to promotion apparently) and so attempt to placate them. Meanwhile their colleagues just learn to bypass them by not including them in emails – because they have become such a bloody liability and genuinely seem to be trying to block progress.

One such staff members behaviour was *so* bad that it was decided that they could not be fired, because if they were, the chances would be much greater that their shenanigans could become public knowledge.

This type of behaviour goes all the way to the top unfortunately. A colleague once told me about an Australian TOTP who screamed at their department's media team that there had not been enough good news stories lately, and that if he didn't get his knighthood, they would be to blame, quite staggering that they are not ashamed to behave in this manner isn't it? And do they have consequences for this behaviour? No.

This is part of the phenomenon of "failing up", let us go for the delightful Urban dictionary definition of this: "Failing Up – The act of performing horribly at your current position, while subsequently getting promoted or advanced to a more predominant position".

Remember Bruce Jobsworth? He was touted as "the man who was *really* running Hooseland" for the previous Government, until it became clear that his real talent was for making such a hash of things during the chair sniffing scandal, he lost them the election. He has failed upwards spectacularly ever since, rewarded with lucrative Board positions, a weekly column in the Hooseland Clarion, and is rumoured to be on his way to a knighthood?? There really seems to be zero (negative) consequences for these people...

When people are faced with a moral or ethical dilemma at work, it's normal to think they only have three options: stay silent, confront the problem on their own, or report them to a Higher-up. Most may end up going for option one as the simplest, but that solves nothing.

So, how can public servants deal with this kind of behaviour? Firstly, they should keep records if they can, so that when the perpetrator denies the wrongdoing, they have evidence. We need to strengthen our ability to confront such questionable behaviour and sometimes this is best done by finding others who no longer want to tolerate this behaviour and making a group complaint. Trying to deal with this behaviour on your own does not work, as history shows nearly 80% of people experience retaliation for reporting this kind of thing. Safety in numbers.

If anyone ever thinks, they are just one bad apple, what harm can they do? Think again. Peer pressure can mean these strong personalities can have a negative peer group pressure effect on the team. I fully recommend every public servant watch The Experimenter movie. It is about Stanley Milgram's investigation as to why ordinary German people had gone along with the Holocaust in World War II. His experiments demonstrated that ordinary people could for the most part easily be pressured into delivering what appeared to be lethal levels of electric shocks to human "victims." Having allies at your side can empower you to act on your values more quickly and decisively than relying on your inner resources alone. And having supportive peers may be especially important for those with more accommodating and conflict-averse personalities.

Unfortunately, the public service has a history of putting people in management with no innate leadership skills or management training. It is common for people with technical competence to apply for a job in a management position in order to keep climbing the ladder. And they may be very good in the area of their technical expertise, but have no people skills, and are not given any training. It's not really their fault; it's a fault in our system.

So much for psychometric testing – it never weeds out the actual psychos in my experience.... Public servants are often just moved up in Hooseland because they are next in the hierarchy.

I know what good looks like and have had some brilliant Higher-ups (the Susan H I told you about earlier was a great example, she was smart, had vision, didn't micromanage and made her team feel valued – like a shining beacon in a dim department. I had to watch her deal with her own psycho Higher-up who was the complete opposite of all of those good things, I have no words for how hard that was to witness...).

A person I met at a party once told me about how they had been working as a Higher-up in the public service but had left due to extreme bullying by their TOTP. They said they had dreaded turning up to work each day so much that it was not uncommon for them to vomit before going to a meeting with this person due to their gas lighting and bullying behaviour. I asked them why they did not whistleblow on this person, and they said they told HR at the time, but nothing happened as HR were just as scared of this person as they were! Crikey.

As public servants, we need to commit as individuals to having values and ethics. So, every time (and trust me, this happens way more often than it should) that a poorly behaved employee is given a promotion to get them out of the immediate reporting line of their Higher-up, it violates our commitment to ethical public service. Sometimes the Hooseland Public Service treats its toxic employees the same way the catholic church treats its paedophile priests – just sweep it under the mat and send them on to another department/parish.... All it takes to lose a good public servant is for them to see a bad one being tolerated.

Yours in service to the public,

Amber Guette (she/her)

You Can't Always Get What You Want

Dear Minister

In the words of Sir Mick Jagger "you can't always get what you want, but if you try sometimes, you get what you need". This month we need to address an elephant in the room for Minister's and public servants – free and frank advice. Now, ever since Lord Meldrum Hoose 'discovered' (apparently all the other people already living here didn't count in a rich, white man's only game of 'I bags it') and imaginatively named this country Hooseland, we Hooselanders have been proud of our reputation for telling the unvarnished truth. Well, it turns out we may need a *teensy* wee bit more of that in our government.

Now clearly this is not aimed directly at you, as you seem fine with hearing the truth, but sadly other Ministers (and a fair portion of our Higher-ups) seem to have a major problem with public servants providing honest advice. It seems the higher up in the pecking order you are, the less likely it becomes that people will feel they can challenge you.

For the professional public servant, providing our Ministers with free and frank advice is not just a good idea – it is a constitutional obligation. Look, we fully respect your election promises (which, let's face it, are often made on the hoof, or without access to all the information needed to ensure they are on the right track), and we are here to action them. But getting that right, and ensuring the public interest is kept paramount, requires good old fashioned honest dialogue.

If we are allowed to provide information in a free and frank manner, we are doing it to ensure the 'no surprises' approach that you demand of us. If you do not want the free and frank, then you cannot always get the no surprises – they often go hand in hand, so it is pretty simple really.

In any organisation, whether it is in our public or private sector, frank and fearless advice is supposed to be part of the service which all capable subordinates owe their Higher-ups. By the same token, the ability to listen and act on such advice is a hallmark of a Minister whose career is likely to survive more than one electoral cycle.

Hooseland Governments and the public need public servants with 'value-seeking imaginations,' rather than just drones who simply do what the Government asks. We are not 'adding value' by simply carrying out your wishes. The new state-of-the-art community health care clinics project is a great example of this. We need to be looking at the real-world conditions that we will have to implement these in.

If we have information that would suggest that a policy will have detrimental long-term effects, or that it will not meet the needs of a large proportion of the public, it is our duty to you *and* the public to point that out and provide helpful alternatives that better meet your desired outcome.

I read somewhere that if a Minister wants to do something that would be a mistake, that it is a constitutional *obligation* to advise them of this at least once, brave and desirable to do so twice, but likely suicidal to do it a third time.

Our advice being ignored is just one of the issues we face in serving Ministers. One of the other issues is the speed with which you expect things to be done. To quote my colleague Anthony, "If they want 'evidence-based, inclusive, joined up, consultative, and outward-facing policy', it will likely take more than a week – but most Ministers seem to expect quality policy advice yesterday".

Some of your colleagues seem to have the impression that public servants are best portrayed by the outdated caricature of the public service we saw in Yes Minister. Of course, this plays right into the hands of those who want to politicise the public service, and fill their offices with political advisers, but in fact, public servants have an excellent record of adjusting quickly to new governments and new policies. More worryingly, there is a risk that political advisers are sometimes a wee bit *too* keen to please their masters and are not providing robust advice that will protect Ministers (and the public) from monumental cockups.

Historically, Ministers that wilfully, blindly and ignorantly ignore evidence-based advice suffer the worst effects. Sure, I get that it can be comforting to surround yourself with nodding heads and soothing agreement, especially when you are new to the role, but history shows that is never the path to greatness. Try to keep a few old warhorses that have seen it all in the office stable, they will also be the ones that will keep their cool and provide wise counsel in an (inevitable) crisis.

It probably seems at times that the brilliant idea you had as the Opposition is met with too much harsh reality when you bring it to the public service to implement. We are used to eager Ministers that know *exactly* how we should achieve their brilliant policy. These Ministers expect us to write them a Cabinet paper based on their idea and their idea only. However, while it may seem like we are just getting in the way, we are actually duty bound as public servants to look at the evidence and see if there any other ways that the objective can be better met. And while your way *may* indeed be the best option, that cannot get in the way of public servants making sure that that is the case.

Delightful though the newly minted from university political advisers in Minister's offices are, they often like to interject themselves into our departmental advice for the Minister, to (no doubt helpfully in their minds) filter out advice that a Minister may seriously need to hear, but that they think is unhelpful, or even possibly embarrassing if it should ever end up on the front page of the Hooseland Clarion.

Political advisers who remove, or potentially even more dangerously at times, modify the department's advice without any consultation with the department, do so in contravention of the Hooseland Constitution. This really should be spelled out for them at the start of their careers to prevent said career being over before it begins....

It amazes me how often various Hooseland governments have tinkered with our public service legislation with the aim of making public servants more accountable for their work. Changes to legislation are all very well and good, but if this is not backed up with support for increased stewardship, and the ability to provide free and frank advice, then our agency has been taken away, and it just becomes more accountability on paper.

Responsibility (which is what you really want) is a moral condition – if you do not have any moral agency over what is being done in your name, you will likely not feel morally responsible, and risk slipping into the coma of becoming the equivalent of a public service zombie – a functionary.

Our ability to fully engage on the matters we are accountable for, *must* have a corresponding level of responsibility. There is no point in lamenting that public servants do not always show a corresponding sense of responsibility for areas of legal accountability if they are not enabled in this way.

Remember that time when the Hooseland Minister of Foreign Relations put their foot in it mightily with the President of a strategically important country? The red-faced Minister's only defence was to say that they had *never* received the advice on it from officials, effectively throwing our lot under the bus. But when it came out in the media after an APFIA request, it was pretty clear that official advice from the department had fully covered that particular bed of thorns.

It also turned out that a certain political adviser in the Minister's office had decided that particular bit of advice was not needed, so they helpfully just deleted it before sending it on to the Minister.... A timely reminder for us in the public service to never *assume* that just because something gets sent to a Minister's office, that the Minister has seen it. The only way we can really be sure is if the advice comes back countersigned by the Minister.

A colleague once tried to kindly remind me that "nobody actually *wants* advice Amber – they want corroboration." So, it is our job to ensure that our free and frank advice gives our Ministers what they need – not just what they want. Like any professional, public servants just need to know their advice has been heard, we accept 100% that in the end, the final decision is always yours as the elected representative.

Yours in service to the public,

Amber Guette

Amber Guette (she/her)

Walk On the Wild Side

Dear Minister

Winter is just around the corner, and I am looking forward to spending some cosy time by the fire reading. Have you read To Kill a Mockingbird by Harper Lee? I think Atticus Finch is an excellent example of what good looks like in a public servant. He remains calm, does not give up, and shows great integrity in the face of huge societal pressure to fold to what those in power want to happen. What would the world be like if every public servant started their day with the following mindset? "You never really understand a person until you consider things from his point of view... until you climb in his skin and walk around in it."

I have been thinking about how important it is in the public service to have that ability to try and see things from another person's point of view. It is not always easy, but there is an easy solution, find the people living in *that* skin and employ them, then they can directly add their point of view to our conversations. We need to make a concerted effort to increase diversity in the Hooseland Public Service, we would all benefit enormously from a more diverse public service that better reflects Hooseland society. Of course, politics could really do with a bit more of that too....

I sighed so loudly when watching question time in the House at work yesterday that my Higher-up asked me what was wrong. I told them that the current Opposition front bench looked like a line up from a 1940's jury – sure, slightly more females than then, but that was the only difference.

It was just straight (well, as far as the public know) white people. Even when it came to a leadership change for your own party, you missed the opportunity to pick the well-known, and widely respected, openly Lesbian Deputy Leader, and put a pretty much unknown politician with little political experience in the top role, so it is not just the public service that needs to try harder....

I was asked once after an interview for a public service role, what was the one thing that I would recommend for improving public service diversity. I replied, "stop hiring yourselves". It seems that unless a conscious effort is made, public servants slip into the habit of hiring their clones – or as close as they can get. This keeps them in their comfort zone, it's not malicious, just an unconscious bias that needs to be addressed.

I can recall walking around one department I worked for and found at least four teams that looked like something out of a science fiction movie. The funniest example was a team that I referred to as the Mr Potato Heads. Five white men all in one team that were variations of Mr Potato Head (tall, bald, glasses, moustache) total lookalikes, with such slight variances in their appearance that I would hate have to pick one out in a police line-up!

There is nothing more depressing than more of the same. Same thinking, same appetite (or lack of it) for risk, same world view – just backing each other up in their excitement to find so many people who agree with them.

Nothing new or innovative comes from the echo chambers this creates. We are often siloed into working 'pods' (unless we are in that other public service hell – hot-desking) which is oddly appropriate as I do sometimes think of them as pod people, peas in a pod.

This should give you a laugh. In one department I worked

in, things got bad gender diversity wise in a team when one of the only two males in their team left for a new job.

They decided as a joke to buy a male blow-up doll and dress it accordingly to balance out (at least visually) the oestrogen vibe in the mostly female team. They cleverly thought that they had ordered one that was not 'anatomically correct' to keep it off the 'Not Safe for Work' spectrum (think Ken Doll smooth), but as is often the case with shopping on the Internet, they got more than they bargained for.

In terms of not being anatomically correct this was definitely the case. Upon un-boxing and beginning the blowing up phase it became rather clear that their overly endowed new colleague was potentially going to raise some eyebrows, let alone trying to get it to fit into the old suit someone had bought from home to attire him in. What ensued was hilarity at the awkward attempts to tie a knot in said appendage. The final solution was duct tape strapping it under the doll, then clothing it as fast as they could so it was trapped in place.

Once suitably clothed, (although some may argue the rainbow-coloured Mohawk wig chosen for Ersatz as he had been named, was not particularly suitable for work, but to be fair they were going for diversity here) they sat him at an empty desk.

He remained there for weeks, providing quiet amusement (important that any fun is quiet in departments as raucous laughter raises eyebrows and mutterings of "who is having fun at work??!"). Several people stopped by after seeing it from the end of the corridor and thinking they had a new person in the team had a good chuckle and as word got around, more people swung by to see him for themselves.

The highlight of Ersatz time in the team was the day the rather shy TOTP stopped by to talk to the Higher-up. The rest of the team had their headphones on and were diligently engaged in calls when he took the Mohawk wig off Ersatz and placed it on his own head – grinning at the Higher-up and then replacing it before the Higher-up could get the attention of any of their team to see what had happened. Needless to say, no one believed them.

On a more serious note, a lack of diversity and the practice of 'hiring yourself', can lead to 'groupthink'. Groupthink then leads to insular decision making as the team share so many assumptions and beliefs that they can ignore or discount evidence to the contrary of those beliefs. The dismissing of those ideas can be so fast and subtle that it is really hard to spot. Psychologists have done studies on conformity, and us human beings are *very* susceptible to peer pressure.

A famous study was done on a group of six strangers – apparently meeting for the first time. In reality, five of the group were in on the experiment. They were told it was a perception exercise and were given two pictures, one was of three lines of different length, and the other was of one line that was the same length as one of the lines in the first picture. The answer was always obvious, but the participants that were in on the experiment went first and always picked a line that was clearly wrong. The real participant went last and gave their answer. On average, about one third (32%) of the participants who were placed in this situation went along and conformed with the clearly incorrect majority on the critical trials. Over the 12 critical trials, about 75% of participants conformed at least once, and only 25% of the participants never conformed.

So why did these participants conform so readily? When they were interviewed after the experiment, most of them said that they did not really believe their conforming answers but had gone along with the group for fear of being ridiculed or thought odd. Apparently, people conform for two main reasons – either because they want to fit in with the group or because they believe the group is better informed than they are.

Anyway, I hope you are having a good month, we have our annual quiz night coming up next Thursday and are busy trying to pick teams that have a wide range of interests so that we can cover off all the categories, yet another lesson in discovering how hard but important diversity in the public service is!

Yours in service to the public,

Amber Guette

Amber Guette (she/her)

Don't You Forget About Me

Dear Minister

Well, winter is here with a vengeance isn't it! To try and heat things up I am going to talk about my favourite topic, and the reason both our jobs exist, the public.

I am starting to become a bit of an astrophysics junkie in my spare time, and I saw something on a documentary last week that made me think of the relationship between the Government, public servants and the public. There are these theoretical places in space called 'Lagrange points', which are the points of equilibrium for an object under the influence of two massive orbiting bodies, say for instance, the earth and the sun. This is the point at which each bodies gravity cancels out the other, and there is no strong pull in either direction. It occurred to me that this sounded like just the right spot for the public service, in equilibrium between the public and the government, or neutral.

When it comes to good public service, political neutrality is definitely at the heart of it, but increasingly, this is too often been more difficult to ensure in reality. One of the problems in Hooseland is that our current arrangements place too strong an emphasis on the relationship between the TOTPs and the Minister.

Another frequent comment I have heard over the years is the growing trend for 'too many Chiefs and not enough Indians' in the public service hampers our ability to service the Hooseland public to the level required. We just seriously need more doers and less talkers on the shop floor. The new state-of-the-art community health care clinics project already seems to be becoming quite 'top heavy' as it is seen as the latest 'spicy' bit of operational policy to be seen doing at CHAOS, and so they all want their name associated with it.

It also seems that increasingly public servants are involved in either securing compliance with our internal performance indicators, or with deflecting members of the public seeking to hold the department to account, thus protecting the department's (and by extension – the Ministers) reputation – so a heady mix of arse covering all round.

So much for all the work we have been doing on Open Government programmes. Openness, while necessary, is not sufficient to ensure inclusive public participation. Inclusion is important to ensure efficacy and equity.

It is time we put the Hooseland public where they belong, front and centre in our work. For example, when we engage the public in consultation on proposed work programmes, like your community health care clinics project, we need to take it a lot more seriously. I saw the numbers on the public consultation for the community health centres and they were *seriously* low. The feedback from those that we even bothered to ask was that they felt their feedback would as usual be ignored, and that it was just another government box-ticking exercise, ouch.

If, as public servants, we can prove that we are here to stand firm, not only against self-interested pressure groups and lobbyists, but also, when necessary, up to Ministers and political advisers who are potentially more concerned with short-term electoral interests than the public interest, we can prove that we are an independent public service, working in the best interest of the community, and we *may* have better luck getting them to engage?

There may be many reasons why it is so hard to get

our people to participate in consultation on public service design and delivery. For example, Hooselanders may *want* to participate, but not be able to due to cultural or language barriers, geographical distance, disability or income. Or people may be able to participate, but not *want* to, perhaps due to a lack of trust, lack of time, or lack of interest.

We need to look at all these barriers as a government and try harder – for the willing this could include removing roadblocks by providing information in multiple languages, bringing the consultation to them, and where necessary, subsidise their involvement.

For the unwilling, we need to think about how we make it more attractive, say make sure the issues are relevant to the audience, give them options for participation, and include on-line and mobile options. We also need to provide the public with adequate *time* to think about their feedback – fast consultation is token at best and can often be more harmful than no consultation as it raises expectations.

We need to be more aware of why public consultation gets such bad press. If we are honest, in the past far too often the decision had already been taken, and the consultation was just 'box ticking'. This was made clear when despite the feedback given, the government just went ahead with its original plan. So, what can we gain from taking the time to do this properly?

Done the right way, engaging Hooselanders (this includes those working in the private sector with specialist knowledge) in public service consultation processes could help heal that lack of trust and even improve legitimacy, impact and buy-in. The decisions that arise from truly open and collaborative processes will be more credible, and when hard choices have to be made, or when disruption may result, will have less political and operational fallout, and more community support.

This has never been truer than with the community health care clinics, which as you will know, have become a bit of a flash point in several towns. Putting this major policy into action will be a good case study if we are given the opportunity to do the consultation properly and will give us a roadmap for community engagement and collaboration in the future.

Speaking of the future, as the government, we can no longer deal with the increasingly complex global and domestic challenges on our own. Issues such as climate change, and the obesity epidemic require massive buy-in from the public if we are to have any chance of addressing them. The sooner we take consultation seriously and get people engaged at the community level, the more quickly we can deliver substantial action and outcomes.

It may be a bitter pill for a politician to swallow, but Hooselanders expect public servants to put the public interest ahead of the governments when exercising our often-considerable powers in bringing new policy to fruition. And happy Hooselanders vote governments back in....

Yours in service to the public,

Amber Guette

Amber Guette (she/her)

Full English Brexit

Dear Minister

Another tough day of operations in the public service. We are working very hard to bring the new state-of-the-art community health care clinics to every town in Hooseland (as per your election promise).

However, I do sometimes wonder if Ministers fully grasp the environment public servants are expected to enact policies in. Because let me tell you, finding places to locate these is turning in to a nightmare – thanks to the 'Not in My Backyard'(NIMBY) brigade.

While almost all of them seem to agree at the individual level that this is necessary, and that improved health outcomes benefit all of society, they still do not want it in *their* neighbourhood. Of course, this is just a minor example of the rampant NIMBYism the western world is facing with leaders going backwards to their silos and building walls and draconian policies to keep the 'other' out, (even though they themselves were once 'other' and their nations are built on 'other').

Sometimes I wish earth could be invaded by aliens whose sole purpose was to give us a wake-up call. What is with humans? Always trying to find ways to divide rather than unite, be it skin colour, gender, religion blah, blah, blah. There is only one race – the human race and we are all stuck on the same planet together, so a few 'Greys' turning up and telling us to get our act together and play nicely or face annihilation could be just the ticket! Yes, I know another one of my space themed rants.

I get it, I really do, people do not like change, but change is the *one* thing they can rely on happening. Paraphrasing Darwin, "It's not the most intellectual of the species that survives; it is not the strongest that survives. It is the one that is able best to adapt and adjust to the changing environment in which it finds itself."

Anyhow, going off track again. What I want to talk about today is how do we get a bunch of people, who individually and who at their hearts are good people that care about better outcomes for those less fortunate than themselves (and many of whom faced with an individual in need of help would no doubt rise to the occasion) to embrace this.

So, what to do? How do we get the community change of heart/mindset, in the face of the Opposition's media beat up about property prices etc, that we need for this really important work, not just to be tolerated, but be seen as a matter of pride to have one of these clinics in your community?

How do we explain to these people that another 'ism' – social universalism – actually lifts nations as a whole? By providing equal access to health, education, and other benefits, we can eventually reach this utopia. It would mean that those born into less fortunate financial circumstances can hope to have the same life outcomes as those that come from families that are prospering. It is universalism in social policy that has successfully resolved class and gender related conflicts in Nordic countries.

Lord, look at me preaching to the converted, I know this is what you want to see too, and the community health care clinics will go a long way to helping achieve this, but it is a long-term solution, not the quick fix some of your media geniuses are touting it as....

I have some thoughts, I have tried raising these as something the department's communications people could do with my Higher-up, but of course as always there is *very* little appetite for risk on that front, so this probably has to come from your office (those Media geniuses perhaps?). Just a thought, but how about *instead* of approaching this in an apologetic manner, while constantly looking over your shoulder to see what the Opposition have to say (by the way, that really needs to stop).

I understand that after years of being the Opposition yourselves it is hard to be the ones in power, but in power you are and if you want to stay there then it may pay to remember, no guts no glory!, what if you take a bold approach to this and lead the narrative instead of reacting to the NIMBYs whipped up by the Opposition and the media all the time? Surely there is someone with widespread respect, some unifying character that you can approach to write an appropriate Op Ed as a 'call to arms' so to speak??

Imagine a nice long op-ed by some much loved, slightly roguish public figure in the Sunday newspaper, someone that gets lots of universal love and approval whenever they pop up in the media? They could start out talking about what life was like during (insert appropriate challenging situation) and how everyone in the community shared what little they had, and how everyone got through because they *all* pulled together....

The next progression would be for them to engage on what they believe to be the modern equivalent of an existential threat facing our communities, the current health crises for example (that was thrown into sharp relief by last year's measles pandemic, and the need for proper universal health care as we face future threats). They could articulate threats we face as a planet – acute in the form of predicted future pandemics, and the chronic ones like the health effects of climate change, as that reality starts to bite harder.

They could then perhaps point out the difference having these new state-of-the-art health clinics will make in the face of those threats? Remind people that these facilities, focused on upstream medicine and supportive social services, will be a hub for the health of the entire community, not just the ambulance at the bottom of the cliff that we Hooselanders have become used to.

They can then perhaps get a little salty in their condemnation of anyone opposed to the new wrap-around community health centres, pointing out the selfishness and short-sightedness of the NIMBY brigade, equating their own situation as one of the many older Hooselanders facing the inevitable increasing range of health issues, that require an increasing range of health services, along with their decreasing desire to have to travel too far to access them.

And for those that will never get it, they can point out that access to these services in (insert appropriate places) communities has actually increased the property values of those lucky enough to be owning property nearby.

Finally, perhaps they can finish with statistics on the tax-payer dollar savings in other areas of government spending as just one of the many benefits of these health clinics. Anyway, as I said, just a thought....

Yours in service to the public,

Amber Guette

Amber Guette (she/her)

Tell It Like It Is

Dear Minister

I think I need to start this month's letter by explaining a theory I have on the relationship between Hooseland Governments and the public service. When I first started in the Hooseland Public Service it seemed clearer, but the waters have become somewhat muddied over time.

I am now going to share with you a metaphor that I think helps explain what I mean. From my perspective, in the past we were more like 'traditional' parents of our child 'the public'. Hooseland Governments had a more paternalistic role, and the public service played 'Mother', and got on with doing all the hands-on work and care. I hope that makes sense so far?

So, with that metaphor in mind, I will attempt to explain how I think things have changed over the decades. These days it feels more like we are divorced parents, sharing custody of our child, or in our case, 'the public'. You have since remarried, and your other half (let's call them the Opposition) thinks they have a say in how our kids are raised too (but let's face it – no – they do not).

One thing never changed, you still seem to hold the purse strings, and the only thing that you and the stepparent (Opposition) have in common, is that you seem to like playing the 'weekend parent', you know, making promises to get approval while we are stuck being the long suffering, put upon, slightly broke, main caregiver. The one who must *try* and keep the balance and long-term well-being of the "child" front of mind, and all the while make possible, where we can, your sometimes very unreasonable promises.

The other slightly tricky bit in our relationship is that you only seem to stick around for a few years, and then the other stricter, let's say, less *generous* stepparent (the Opposition in this scenario remember) jumps in and confuses the hell out of the kids (and makes a lot more work for us), by coming up with a whole *new* set of rules. They (the public) are children after all, so while they love the idea of more pocket money, once they realise that they must buy *everything* they need out of it they are not quite so impressed.... Of course, that never works, we both know they are not great at budgeting and prioritising their money, so there is never enough to go around, and they start missing out, and then vote your party back in again, and so the wheel keeps turning...

Righto, so leaving my metaphors behind for now, it is always good for all three of us to bear in mind that the public interest ranges much wider than any Governments, and that it is the job of public servants to keep putting these wider perspectives in the Governments view, all the while of course, carrying out the lawful instructions of the Government of the day. So, we diligently get on with the business of writing 'Briefings' and 'Policy Papers' to ensure you have all the facts in front of you as you make decisions.

This has always required public servants to raise the risks and downsides to proposed policies, and offer constructive ways through, so that the Government's objectives are best met. In the past that was just taken as read, but these days Governments can seem a little *too* keen to insert themselves before we have even provided said advice, and at times even attempt to change it! Which if you think about it, doesn't really make it *our* advice anymore does it?

Look, I am not saying it was ever easy to provide advice

that was not in line with the Government's objectives, and it always took a rather skilled public servant, with confidence in the advice being offered, as well as plenty of experience in delivering unsolicited advice.

I would be wrong to say that historically governments have always been receptive, or happy with the advice they have been given, but (and this is a big but), they at least respected the role of the public servant, and their department, to provide it, before they completely ignored it.

I get it, Hooseland's four-year electoral cycle tends to focus governments on the short term. But the public service has a duty of stewardship, we are tasked with looking ahead and providing advice to the best of our abilities, around the future challenges and opportunities Hooseland is likely to face.

So, in those Briefings and policy papers, it is our job to tell you what you need to hear, even if it is not what you want to hear. And, again, it is totally up to you as the democratically elected Government of Hooseland, to do with that advice as you please. If you stop and think about it, it is in *your* best interests that the public service is *not* politicised. I am sure that during your time in opposition you would have been greatly aggrieved if you had thought we were being subservient and allowing *that* Government to interfere in our provision of free and frank advice....

Well, I am telling you now that at times they did, but before you get too excited at their gall, and the only reason I am sharing this information with you at all, is because the *same thing* appears to be happening on your watch... this is despite the fact that during your time in opposition you stated that "Public servants have come to ask Ministers: "What advice would you like Minister?"

You then implied that public servants were being

negligent and serving only Ministers, not the public who in a democracy are supposed to be the ultimate client. And yet I was advised yesterday by one of our Private Secretary's in your office that a senior political adviser has now firmly overstepped the mark by insisting that it is *their* job to decide what you need to hear from CHAOS.

They took exception to one of our Briefings and contacted the office of our TOTP to ask for it to be withdrawn and noted that they had some changes they wanted made before it went back to the Minister... as this had already been signed out by our TOTP this was a serious breach (or as our department's Private Secretary so eloquently put it, "a clusterfuck...".

Governments *must* be willing to take free and frank advice – this kind of behaviour can have a disturbing effect on the public service due to the power imbalance.

It was widely agreed in the public service that under the last Government a worrying habit had developed of departments trying to anticipate what they *thought* the Government *wanted* to hear, rather than just giving them the facts of the matter. And it seems that is not changing – I won't lie, this worries the heck out of me, as I was so sure that integrity levels in a more progressive government would see a marked improvement on this kind of interference?? This is not the only example I have heard from other departments, but maybe now that you have been made aware of it, you can raise it with your colleagues?

We have been advising our groups Higher-up that in order to protect the department from this kind of thing we need to ensure that all our advice be given in writing. If it has to be given verbally, then at the very least a written record of that should be kept.... Sunlight is the best disinfectant, and if certain people know records are being kept that can then be discovered under Hooseland's APFIA, then it *might* just have a civilising effect on their decision making.

Back to the metaphor at the start of this letter – if the kids see us behaving badly then they will think if it is good enough for us, it is good enough for them. Monkey see – monkey do. Further to that, we need to not just be seen to be doing the right thing, we actually need to do it!

Yours in service to the public,

Amber Guette (she/her)

I Think It's Going to Rain Today

Dear Minister

Happy one year anniversary on the job! To celebrate I am going to share with you today some stories about the best of our public servants.

The old cliche 'Not Every Hero Wears a Cape' happens to be true in the public service, and I have been privileged to witness some of this everyday heroism, and the empathy and commitment to the public that they bring to the job. A lot of this behaviour stems from why Hooselanders are motivated to work in the public service to begin with. Trigger warning, for you to understand these everyday Hooseland heroes you will first need to understand the environment which they have to rise above in order to shine.

Did you read *The Catcher in The Rye* at school? I did. I know Salinger doesn't appeal to everyone, but I loved it. It really connected with my 12-year-old budding sense of social justice.

At that age you start to realise the world is not necessarily a fair place, and that maybe you needed to decide where you stand on things. I remember really liking the bit where Holden spoke about his dream of being in a big field of rye grass with a whole bunch of little kids who were running around and playing in the grass, unaware of a big cliff at the edge of the field.

Holden's dream job was to be the person who had to catch any child who looked like they were going to go over the edge. I decided then that would be where I would stand.

I wanted to be a catcher in the rye and help stop people falling over the cliff (metaphorically speaking of course I get chronic hay fever and all that long grass sounds like a nightmare!).

Anyway, that's why I was attracted to public service. Trust me, a lot more public servants joined out of motivation to make a real difference than many would believe. They joined to help improve the lives of ordinary Hooselanders, working to help those who fell through the system – the homeless, the food insecure, the unemployed, and to help provide effective health, welfare and education systems to stem the rising tide of 'have nots' in Hooseland.

While writing this letter I thought I should see what the research said about what motivated public servants to choose the profession. There is certainly plenty out there on this topic – even whole 'theories' of public service motivation. To be honest it kind of made for sad reading. The research backs up that many of us do enter for very altruistic reasons, wanting to make a difference and contribute to the world by serving the public. And guess what? For many it just gets beaten out of them.

At the really bad end of the spectrum some may come across bullies, discrimination, or the odd sociopath, playing with them like a cat with a mouse. Or some find themselves taking a long, soul-destroying path to disillusionment, stuck in a system full of red tape that blocks their efforts to make a difference, or that workplace hierarchies frustrate their ability to do their best work.

Even just discovering some of your colleagues are careerists looking out for number one, and ready to throw you (or the public interest) under the nearest passing bus, can be enough for them to leave. Worse still – they may have been broken, but stay, switch off, do the job like a cog in the machine, and try to find their fulfilment outside of their work.

Life can be pretty precarious for many Hooselanders, and that is something we come face to face with daily as public servants. The public likely think that we do not care and carry out our work in a detached manner and for the above reasons for some I guess that is true. But not for all. There are many public servants out there with real heart and empathy. Let me introduce you to some of them.

The first one was Jessie, a young graduate who had been working in the Hooseland Public Service for eight months. Her job was simple enough, drafting letters in response to communication from the public. I found her crying at her desk one day and asked what was wrong, she proceeded to tell me about a letter from an old woman with cancer living in government run housing. In order for her to get the care she needed, she had to move to another town, where she has no friends or family, and the place we were moving her to would not let her take her cat.

The letter went on to say the cat has been the woman's companion and source of comfort for the past 12 years, and that she was worried that her cat would be put down if left behind. I agreed that this was very sad and gently asked her what she thought we could do to help? She stopped crying and stood up saying, "We must find a way to fix this! It is *unbearably* sad to think of this woman being so sick and being worried about her beloved moggy." She announced that *she* would look after the cat and take it to visit the bereft owner on weekends. And no doubt she would have.

Fortunately, we found an even better solution and managed to get an exemption for the cat as an 'emotional support' animal so that it could continue to stay with the owner. No one can accuse Jessie of being nameless, faceless or a bureaucrat.

A colleague had a call once from the department's Private Secretary in your office – he was rather agitated, and it turned out he had a letter from a 12-year-old, who was trying to navigate our complex health system to get support for his bi-polar mum. His Dad had left, and in his absence the child had taken on the weight of looking out for his mum.

The usually unflappable Private Secretary demanded the number of *someone* in the department who could DO SOMETHING IMMEDIATELY to help this kid and his mum. He could have done the usual pat response about this not being an issue for the Minister to get involved in, as it was an operational matter, and to fob him off that he would pass the letter on to officials at CHAOS, but he didn't. And, yes, they found someone who could help and got them to ring and get the boy's address so they could send a Health Assessor around that day. When these chasms open in Hooselanders lives and a public servant is faced with the immediacy of human suffering, they can switch gears, and magic can happen.

Perhaps you are thinking that is all very nice, but that level of service is not sustainable for everyone? But in being there to act these public servants not only brought light into the lives of the people they helped, but they also made a real difference to how much more motivated and rewarded they felt as public servants. We can learn from that.

In preparation for this letter, I asked my team for examples of when they have seen public servants go above and beyond for the public. Anthony told me a very sad story he had heard about in our claims department, of an elderly man (let's call him Rex because I had an Uncle Rex and he was feisty) and his battle to get CHAOS compensation for his wife's paralysing injury at work, just as she was about to join him for their joint retirement adventures.

By the time this particular public servant came across Rex he had spent the past three years campaigning to get (thanks to a technical hitch in the form of red tape) what should have rightfully been theirs all along. Tragically, his wife had passed away in the intervening years, and Rex had been diagnosed as terminally ill, and the department had finally changed the small piece of legislation that had caused him and his wife so much grief.

This of course, was not retrospective so Rex would gain nothing from it, other than the knowledge that he had saved others from going through their awful experience. He wrote to say he was glad to hear that it had finally been changed, that he was dying, and that the department would probably be happy to hear, as they likely thought he was a pain in the neck.

This deeply distressed the public servant, who was a kind man and hated to think anyone thought that public servants would be pleased to hear someone who had fought for what was right, was going to die without any recompense. He knew he could not do anything to change what had happened, so, he did something that would likely have gotten him in to trouble if he had been caught.

The public servant's daughter went to university in the city that this man lived in, so he rang her, and gave her the man's address and asked her to write the following in a card to be delivered along with a gift basket of food he had ordered along with a bottle of good whisky: "Congratulation's on the win – you beat the buggers! This is to thank you for your grit and determination in setting right a wrong. You have reached the rank of hero in the war against unfairness". It was sent anonymously of course.

So, you see Minister, the milk of human kindness still flows amongst us, I think empathy and the ability to walk a mile in someone else's shoes should be a Key Performance Indicator for public servants. But the Hooseland public should not have to "rely on the kindness of strangers" – the system needs to take this human approach to all its policies and processes. Time for a spring clean me thinks. On that note spring showers so don't forget your umbrella tomorrow.

Yours in service to the public,

Amber Guette

Amber Guette (she/her)

Honesty

Dear Minister

Now that we are past the one-year mark for the new Government it is probably a good time to reflect on how things are going from a public servant's viewpoint (and also probably time to stop referring to your Government as 'new' as well).

So, as you know there are five public service principles that we are expected to adhere to here in Hooseland. These are to be politically neutral, to provide free and frank advice, to have merit-based appointments, to have transparent government, and to provide stewardship of resources for our public. All these principles will likely all be addressed in the course of my letters, but this letter is focused on the fourth principle – transparent government.

The public want honest Ministers who live up to their election promises supported by public servants that *stick* to the above principles and therefore help to keep them honest.

One of my witty friends sent me a meme the other day, "The mightiest of weapons is truth, and everyone knows you are not allowed to enter a government building with a weapon...". It was funny but way too often it is true. We are not talking about *blatant lies* here for the most part, it is more about fudging things, or misinterpreting the question/request on purpose to avoid an honest response, hiding information that may be deemed embarrassing.

The worst two things in terms of honesty in my opinion are when firstly, a Minister or department, mistakenly gets the wrong information out into the public realm, but instead of correcting the information (and this is borderline insane) tries to back engineer the situation to make the wrong information *technically* right.

Or, when a Minister makes a policy announcement on the hoof, without vetting it via their department first, and rather than 'embarrass' (or more likely anger) the Minister by pointing out the evidence shows that this will never work, the department tries desperately for months to bash a square peg into a round hole. It all sounds rather exhausting and pointless, doesn't it? Well quite frankly it is!

As you will already know about four years ago the previous Government signed Hooseland up to the Global Transparent Government Pledge (apparently only after a *lot* of peer pressure from the other allied countries that had already signed up...). The point of this exercise was to encourage a shift towards more transparent governments pro-actively making information available to the public, not just when they request it under freedom of information Acts like our APFIA. The fact being that the people holding all the information, hold all the power – and it is time to put the power back where it belongs, in the hands of the public. It is no longer acceptable for governments to call themselves a 'democracy' just because they get voted in once every four years.

Despite the previous Government signing us up, not a lot has happened on that front yet. There was some tinkering at the edges by a few keen public servants back at the start, (clearly they thought this was their time to shine) but I heard on the public service grapevine that the Minister in charge of that particular department at the time had a rather allergic reaction to the actions their research proposed we commit to, as part of our Global Transparent Government

Pledge, and quietly stalled that effort...

Back to the present day – you can imagine how excited I was when you promised in the elections that you would transform Hooseland into a shining example of "transparent and fully democratic government" that would really stretch our Global Transparent Government Pledge commitments, by improving public consultation, pro-actively releasing information, and increase the visibility of accountability measures. Fabulous!

Between you and me, there is quite a lot to fix, and I have a comprehensive wish list as you will soon see, but I know many public servants who would jump at the chance to work on this (a lack of it affects our reputation as public servants and fixing it would seriously help raise morale). But for this to *actually work* it will need some very strong leadership from the top and a focus on a culture of integrity not compliance.

A lot of the problem with the 'honesty factor' in the public service has been due to the pressure on the TOTPs to protect Ministers (and let's be honest, by association themselves) from bad press. This pressure when it is exerted further down the human caterpillar becomes paranoid risk averseness on the part of the Higher-ups, which translates into pressure on public servants to pre-empt anything they think will set off their Higher-up.

I saw a Hooseland Public Service review a few years back that stated many public servants, and in fact anyone receiving government funding, were afraid to speak out on anything that might reflect poorly on the Government. That is definitely not in the public interest, surely, we need the voices of those that have experience at the coalface when it comes to important public matters? Should that not be expected given the investment the public make in these services? We are not talking about 'airing dirty laundry' (although sunshine is the best disinfectant...) but contributing to the conversation where they can add value.

We could really do with some new policy around the whole 'no surprises' thing too while we are at it. I understand that you need to know what we are sending out in your name, and to be given a heads up if we are releasing information requested under the APFIA that is not yet in the public domain, but I am pretty sure we are *not* supposed to be letting your political advisers make changes to our advice before it 'officially' lands on your desk.

Surely if we are apolitical then our independent, evidence-based advice should be exactly that? Of course, from that point on you have every right to provide feedback, but that feedback should also be on the public record. That is how democracy works.

While we are on the topic, let's take a look at what things might look like in Hooseland if we *really* took the whole transparency thing seriously. A starter for ten of course would be the long awaited (as noted in the Truth and Freedom letter last summer) overhaul of the APFIA, and perhaps some government announcements on your desire to see free and frank advice from an apolitical public service?

Another shift in behaviour that would really help to fulfil the Government's election promise, would be to seek a cross-government mandate to make it clear that public servants, and others funded by government, not only have the right to speak up on matters of public interest, but as they are funded by the public, an obligation. That would *really* prove that you are changing the culture from one of opacity to one of openness.

Also, how about exploring what other democracies

outside of Hooseland are doing around public consultation settings for new laws and policies? Sometimes it feels like these are being handled as back-room deals. Yes, I know that good consultation takes time, but by taking that time we will gain more trust from the public, strengthen legitimacy as a democracy and develop better laws and policies. Sounds like a good investment to me.

On the bright side, the new proposed whistleblowing laws are a great start, and I am super pleased that we are finally going to make it punishable by law to retaliate on a whistleblower. It was a bit like watching a train wreck in slow motion when under the previous Government the Hooseland Forestry Board sued a whistleblower, who had alerted the public to their carbon credit corruption, for bringing them into 'disrepute'!

However, the proposed new whistleblowing laws do not go far enough based on international best practice, and we Hooselanders do like to be the best, don't we? There are still no guarantees that the whistleblower's identity will be protected, and the laws are still limited to internal whistleblowing, not to whistleblowing in public or in the media, so that definitely needs extending.

And finally, given the scandals in recent years around political parties and election financing, now would be a great time for the Government to make the most of being in power and get this sorted at pace.

We need more transparency around the funding of political parties (rather murky business at present), while we all understand that money matters in politics, it should *not* be allowed to buy access to decision-making power.

We need a level playing field for all parties competing in elections, and a transparent way to ensure they are independent and not beholden to outside influences (speaking of which, let's add a publicly available register of lobbying to the list too!).

Yours in service to the public,

Amber Guette (she/her)

Don't Come Around Here No More

Dear Minister

This month's letter comes to you on behalf of the public. This will not surprise you as I am sure you get plenty of feedback from your friends, but I can tell you that mine *do not* have a problem with giving me free and frank feedback on the things we are getting wrong as a public service.

I recently read an article in a science magazine that looked into why, of all the types of humans that have existed, homo sapiens are the only ones left. They came up with a theory that it was most likely our *kindness* as a species that ensured the survival of homo sapiens versus the other hominids around back then. Apparently, our ability to work together, show empathy and (unsurprisingly) our emotional neediness caused us to connect to others in our group. On first glance all that could be seen as a vulnerability, but the scientists say it could have given us the edge by growing our communities and ability to cooperate. On that note I want to introduce you to my childhood friend Patty.

Patty definitely comes with a trigger warning – *never* mention CHAOS and our departments visits to her kindergarten with all our possibly well-meaning, but often misplaced, underfunded and way too late and difficult to access community health interventions.

This woman is brilliant, she is a passionate and dedicated Head Teacher of a Kindergarten, and I am proud to call her my friend. She is very invested in the well-being of the children, and the mostly migrant community they come from. But she often tells me that like many others, she is worn down by the uphill battle she faces when advocating for the most vulnerable on their roll. She is frustrated and concerned for the children she knows need help that they cannot access.

She told me yesterday she was in at work (it was Sunday) and she had been scrolling through all the emails and documentation from her attempts to engage with the department. They tell a story of great effort from her over the past ten years to engage with the multiple attempts by the department for input on policy. Yet from what she can see, none of that has *ever* translated into significant improvements for the frontlines, and the issues that they raised with the department are still as relevant today, ten years later.

Okay, so all that doesn't sound very hopeful or positive, but that's an unfiltered insight into how our public are experiencing the government's attempts at intervention.

The honest truth is that our Child Health Early Intervention Service is letting them down. The waiting list for assessments are long, and since many of the parents are immigrants to Hooseland, they do not know what services their child is eligible for, so Patty and the other teachers feel they must help navigate the system on their behalf. And it can take up to eight months to even get an assessment, leaving a big gap in the opportunity to reap the benefits of early intervention.

She told me once that one of the health assessors even told her that CHAOS actually *forbids* our staff from talking to teachers about its services, and she questions whether we are deliberately working to lower expectations and therefore place responsibility back onto the kindergartens and families? Any changes in our policy over the years are seen by her as "just moving the deck chairs around on the Titanic".

Patty tells me the problem is not with our health assessors, they are good people dedicated to helping provide successful health outcomes, but they are underpaid and overworked and when they leave, they are often not replaced or, even when they are there is no handover. That then means the already very busy teachers must start from scratch in building a relationship with new adviser as they come to grips (all over again) with the needs of the children.

Apparently after the last health assessor left, it took *two months* for a new one to be appointed, so any progress with the children was stalled. When we finally provided a new health assessor it took them months to catch up...

Patty says the biggest problem is that the funding no longer meets the needs or the numbers of children requiring help. She is yet another Hooselander that has been worn down by the system and disheartened by the big delays in response to her emails, the unanswered phone calls, and the push back from the public service when she is trying very hard to get help on turning (what start out as) small problems around, so that a child can get back on track as soon as possible.

I know there are many more just like her trying hard to work within a broken system and banging their heads against a brick wall. Surely, we can find a way to better serve these children and their communities.

Of course, you understand that the public's experience of our services should always be important to Governments and the public service. It is *your* role as politicians to respond to the public's priorities, and *our* role as public servants to deliver on their expectations. This has become more important now than ever in a time of spending restraint, and 'doing more with less'. We need to be making sure that we are making informed choices about how we allocate resources and delivering in a way that has the most impact. As Patty would say, just because you *can* do something, doesn't mean it's sensible in any way to do it.

You are probably wondering what I have done to try and improve things at CHAOS, given that I am so quick to tell you where things are going wrong. I have taken Patty's concerns to the people that work in this area in CHAOS, and none of it is news to them. They tell me they know the system is broken, and that this makes their job very hard, but that the Higher-ups do what the Minister asks and are not big on them showing initiative and pro-actively *telling* the Minister what the problems are. And even if they do, it is highly unlikely to make it past the political advisers in your office unless it fits with your current policy narrative.

A recent survey on the Hooseland Public Service found that only three out of ten Hooselanders trusted public services, so Patty is not alone in her concerns. To rebuild trust, the Hooseland Public Service needs to foster a culture in which public servants do not just comply with rules and pay lip service to shared values, but ensure our combined actions result in a public service that is trustworthy. Greater trust, in turn, will generate openness, public participation, and genuine partnerships with communities. I know we can do better as a public service, and happily as the (newish) Government, this is what your party promised we *would* do.

It is common knowledge that for every dollar we spend on early childhood programmes we get a five-fold return on that investment. High quality early childhood programs promote healthy development, and they generate savings by reducing the need for more expensive interventions later in a child's life. So, we *all* benefit.

I remain hopeful that we can use the new community health centres as a hub for better meeting the needs of our public, and that these will be based in the parts of towns that need them most, as per the research from the department. We have yet to hear your feedback on the findings, but I trust your political advisers are all over that....

Yours in service to the public,

Amber Guette

Amber Guette (she/her)

Keep Me Hanging on the Telephone

Dear Minister

This year is flying by – it is tax time again, but good luck getting anyone on the phone at the tax department... In honour of the long-suffering public trying to access our services and being put 'on hold' I thought this month we would have a look at that extra special torture – trying to call a government department.... This might not be a letter you would expect to get from me as this may seem quite trivial to you, but it is often the first contact the public make with the public service, so it warrants further investigation.

Fun fact, in Hooseland the public service deals with over 234 million calls a year, so let's consider what message we are sending the public when they call us? I have often wondered what the people that create the call waiting content are *thinking*?

Any research into the experience of being put on hold, must surely begin with our own department, CHAOS. We apparently have the dubious accolade of leaving people hanging on the telephone the longest, Steve from IT said our hold times seem to range from between 15 minutes to half an average adult lifetime. We are told the appalling music is there to keep people on the line until their call can be answered, but I seriously doubt that. Let's be honest, it's not meant to keep people on the line, it's meant to make people hang up. Less people waiting on the lines means less people that need help with something right?

If it was truly designed to keep people on the line, then why on earth would you have Celine Dion's 'My Heart Will Go On' played badly on the pan flute, with extra static, over and over – seriously? Surely association with the sinking of the titanic is not something government departments should be doing.

How can the aim of this be anything *other* than a concerted effort to make the listener lose the will to live and hang up? Sure, some creative souls may choose to make the best of the wait and start choreographing TikTok dances, but let's face it, for normal people, being on-hold just means precious time wasted. No one rings government departments for fun. It is usually a last-ditch attempt to deal with a problem that the FAQs on your website had not figured on, or to request urgent assistance from an actual human being as not everybody has access to the internet.

Adding insult to injury the sound quality of on hold music is more often than not horrendous. It often sounds like a crappy, staticky radio that is slightly off station is being blasted down the phone, I very much doubt that Shazam could tell you what the original music even was.... Steve informs me it is because a telephone line only carries a tiny amount of sound frequency range that works for the frequency that humans talk at, but not the much wider range of frequencies that music has.

You could be forgiven for thinking that perhaps after more than 50 years, public service on-hold music would have adapted to this change in technology. But no, we are sticking with music quality that makes the public feel assaulted. And our call centres wonder why the public are so grumpy by the time they pick up after 27 minutes of that....

I was on hold with the Hooseland Department of Motor Vehicle Licensing for over an hour the other day. They played the same 40 second muzak loop, and in between each loop inserted that dial tone leading to someone droning on about changes to traffic laws... it was like being stuck in the seventh circle of hell.

If you were wondering why government departments can't play some catchy, upbeat, commercial Hooseland music, it's because it is a much more *expensive* option given that it attracts license fees, and our meagre budgets dictate that we could never do anything as extravagant as that.

What if we introduced some humour to show that we are not the pompous arses the public often think we are and play muzak that hints that perhaps we are in on the joke. I did a quick canvas of my team for suitable choices and they came up with the following: The Eagles – 'I Can't Tell You Why', Blondie's – 'Hanging on the telephone', Rolling Stones – 'I Can't Get No Satisfaction', Eric Carmen – 'All By Myself', Tom Petty and the Heartbreakers – 'The Waiting', Roy Orbison – 'Communication Break Down', The Clash – 'Should I stay or Should I go'. Not a bad start...

Of course, the *ultimate* (and obvious) solution would be to put an end to on hold muzak forever, by playing catch up with the private sector and offering the public the option of receiving a call back.... Very much the least annoying option.

Have you ever tried calling your own office in Parliament by the way? Whoever selected 'duelling banjos' as the on-hold muzak for the Parliamentary switchboard is a bonafide genius in my opinion.

Yours in service to the public,

Amber Guette

Amber Guette (she/her)

My Colleagues Respect Me

Dear Minister

I hope you enjoyed the extra day off last week for Labour Day. Having an extra day got me thinking that one of the bonuses of your new career must be not having to deal with HR. You are voted in, not recruited, and the Parliamentary Administration Department takes care of all the recruitment etc for your office. Bliss.

I know that if you asked the Hooseland public to identify the most distrusted group within the public service, they would say it was our Media and Comms people. But if you ask a public servant the same question, pretty sure that most would say HR. Today's letter looks into why that might be and what can be done about it.

Let's take a brief look at the history of Human Resources in the Hooseland Public Service. Decades ago, "HR" were called "Personnel", and it felt like their role was to support the structures around the work of the departments. To ensure that the system of meritocracy worked, that good process was in place for recruitment, progression and retention of capable public servants. This model saw the employees as an asset.

In more recent years in Hooseland, you get the impression that "HR" is there to form a protective layer, guarding the Higher-ups from the employees, or as Steve from IT puts it, "running a protection racket for Higher-ups". This model sees employees as a source of liability.

In my simplified view every role or function within a

department should have a balance of autonomy, authority and accountability. Sadly, in HR usually they have spades of the first two, but none of the last one. HR now seem to have way too much power within most departments.

In an ideal world we would all be blessed with good HR professionals – enablers and true business partners. In the current not ideal one we are sadly sometimes stuck with the bad ones, Steve says that the bad ones fall into two camps, firstly the checklist chasers, (these people are so risk averse that they still wouldn't cross the street on a walk signal), or the second camp, much scarier, these are the ones that are actively gaming the system to keep Higher-ups happy, and thus themselves employed. These ones are not above ruining the career of anyone that gets in their way as an added bonus.

Let me paint you a picture of what the first camp looks like, bearing in mind this is just how things work, with no malice aforethought on their behalf.

Imagine you are a diligent Higher-up in the public service. You have inherited a new team, and you are carefully planning your team structure and budgets and realise, that to *really* get things humming, you need two advisor level staff (more budget friendly) with more project co-ordination skills, rather than two senior advisor level ones, whose job description is heavily weighted on strategic advice. So being a good Higher-up and seeing that this will deliver better results for both the department, *and* the public, you set about trying to change both the classification, and the level for the roles. Sounds simple enough right? Wrong.

You go to HR and explain what you want to do, to get the jobs resized and reclassified because it makes better sense for the work that needs to be done. You provide ample evidence of why this is the case, you will then be put through exhaustive interviews with the HR classification team, and chances are they will come back to you offering an even *worse* classification than what you started with. Insanity.

I asked my calm, considered colleague Anthony what he thought of HR – he sighed heavily and asked if I was referring to 'Human Remains' as he called them, and then he recalled one particularly 'amusing' situation when he was working in a department that was undergoing a major, and rather confusing, restructure. Although there had been a 'consultation' document circulated with the affected group, and they had provided very clear feedback on said document, it was clear that the restructure was a foregone conclusion, and no amount of common-sense and in-depth thinking offering much better solutions was going to budge it. This was clearly not best practice as it was being done *to* them, not *with* them.

He attended a particularly tense meeting, where the unpopular, and socially awkward Higher-up in charge of the restructure was providing the final response on what the restructure would involve, and the head of HR had been wheeled out to support them at the meeting.

He described how the head of HR stood shoulder to shoulder with the Higher-up, eyeballing them all like a Deputy Principal at a school assembly does when the Principal is speaking, trying to intimidate them so that they would 'behave', basically treating them like children not to be trusted as they had dared to make their opinions known in their free and frank submission.

He had been with that department for almost 17 years and said he never saw the same hiring process twice. Almost like the rules change with every vacancy....

Meanwhile back at CHAOS, our lot in HR seem to have been taking tips from Procurement, and only give out limited information on the steps needed to get someone new recruited, not the whole process. It is like their spidey senses tell them that *if* we know the whole process, we will just circumvent the completely unnecessary steps... (correct).

So, instead, it becomes here's steps 1-3, now go away and leave us alone. Then when you get back to them with that, you will get step 4, and so on... you will also more than likely have to deal with multiple advisors in the course of this process. By the time you get to meet advisor number 2 or 3, they suddenly find out that everything done by the *previous* advisor was wrong for your particular recruitment request, and you will have to start over from scratch. It is for all of these reasons and more that the entire process can span months, or if you are really unlucky, years.

On a lighter note, my favourite HR moment was in a compulsory 'resilience' training session that the wise heads in HR had decided we needed to do to improve morale (zero awareness of the extra stress not being able to get on with our mounting pile of work was having on the team).

Helpfully, Paula from HR (voted by the team as public servant most likely to get our blood pressure up) was chosen to lead this exercise. We were given a 'Sheep Scale'(I kid you not) that depicted nine pictures of sheep (interesting choice of animal for public servants) each representing an emotion or state of being (so we were told – can be hard to pick emotion with sheep).

We were asked to pick which sheep we associated with the most right now. Sheep no.4 had a yellow bucket on its head, and despite this being done individually, not as a group, *everyone* in the team picked that one and the muffled laughter grew louder as it was clear we were all a "4".

Paula was *not* impressed and eyeballed us all with her steely eye and said, "I am sensing hostility", to which Steve from IT replied "Really, because I am sensing bullshit". Well, that was it – we just lost it and nearly fell off our chairs laughing. No doubt he will be written up (again) for that particular piece of 'free and frank' feedback. Safe to say, Steve did not have to pay for his drinks at the obligatory trip to the pub that follows any team building exercise in the public service....

As I explained in the Psycho Killer letter last autumn, everyone in the Hooseland Public Service has a story about a colleague with a proven record of incompetence going back decades, who continues to be promoted. That does not happen in a vacuum and HR along with Higher-ups need to take responsibility for not making merit-based appointments.

Ultimately however, it is the TOTP (Board included) who are to blame – they are the only ones that can put HR in its place. HR culture should be driven from the top and reflect the stated values of the Hooseland Public Service – as we prepare for the future, we need strong, competent, emotionally intelligent and resilient public servants. Perhaps the next annual restructure in the search for efficiencies could focus on HR and leadership roles?

Yours in service to the public,

Amber Guette

Amber Guette (she/her)

I Am Good at Organising Meetings

Dear Minister

What glorious weather we are having – I see you have been on holiday, good for you! Always hard to get back into the work once you return, isn't it? Especially those interminable meetings that seem to fill up the calendar like it was a game of Tetris, and every available spot *must* be filled....

Did you know that the correct collective noun for public servants is a 'meeting' of public servants? Have you ever left a meeting and thought, gosh, I wish that had gone on longer? No? Me neither.

I have however, sat there quietly tracing the outline of my hand in order to play a (safe for the public service) version of the knife game using a ballpoint pen. There is of course zero risk of hurting yourself as you stab the pen faster and faster around the outline. Pretty silly I can hear you thinking, but if you saw the state of the piece of paper by the end of the meeting you would see that it was a very sensible way to play it. If I had been playing the real game, I would have been fully incapacitated....

I have been pondering why Hooseland public servants torment each other with endless meetings?? I mean, a well organised meeting with an actual goal that has a meaningful outcome can be a thing of beauty, but I have been in such painfully, boring and unproductive meetings in the past I once even started to fantasise about whether you could *actually* kill yourself with a ballpoint pen. I even Googled it one day (in a meeting), and someone has taken the time to document 101 ways that you *can actually* kill yourself with a ballpoint pen (more than likely while they sat in a meeting too...)

I think it's more the haphazard way meetings are conducted, not just the sheer number of them, that annoys most public servants. Bizarrely, given the amount of time involved in meetings, I have never seen "how to run a meeting" training in the multiple on-line training options most Hooseland departments offer public servants.

An effective meeting should really involve only the absolutely necessary people required to make an informed decision. Instead, way too many meetings involve entire teams and last far too long. Consulting relevant people is, of course, common sense. Yet, bless them, public servants seem to think they need to try to reach a 'consensus' on all decisions! This leads to the whole point of meetings being to hear from everybody, rather than make, or communicate a decision.

Susan H, (the excellent Higher-up I told you about in the Psycho Killer letter), seriously impressed me when I went to my first meeting with her. A well-meaning Higher-up had organised a meeting on the project for the new state-of-the-art community health centres, and it came complete with a cast of thousands (well, 47 but seriously!?).

In lieu of the usual awkward getting everyone to introduce themselves, she started with an even more awkward – what is your role and why do you need to be here? By the time she got to the 9th person, people all over the room were getting up to leave, knowing full well they had no real reason to be there. Hilarious, but effective and we got on with a jolly good meeting of the 12 people left in the room. Genius!

Another one of her endearing qualities was to have one-on-one meetings as a 'walking meeting' (partially because we had zero meeting rooms, but also because she was so busy, she needed to be at the next meeting the minute your one with her had ended). Of course, this only works if there are only two to three people in the walking meeting, (although it would be hilarious to see a 'meeting' of public servants of varying fitness walking and yelling at each other as they jockey for position....)

Stuck in unproductive meetings public servants get innovative in ways of trying to find something interesting to focus their attention, so that they do not nod off in the meeting. Steve from IT has been known to email us before a group meeting with instructions on that day's game of 'buzzword bingo' where we would engage in tallying up all of the cliches speakers would use. It provided light relief, but also ensured we engaged in the meeting, if only to win the game....

According to a study reported by the Hooseland Clarion, the average public servant sends three emails for every 30 minutes of meeting time. If you think that is bad – apparently virtual meetings make it even easier to zone out. The same study found that 43% of virtual meeting attendees checked social media during meetings, and that 65% were on mute doing other work (guilty as charged your honour).

It gets worse, as there are ongoing repercussions for bad meetings. Apparently how public servants feel about the effectiveness of meetings correlates directly to their job satisfaction. So instead of improving communication and collaboration, bad meetings undermine those things. Why are these clearly bored public servants so disengaged you may ask?

Turns out the report had the answers to that as well.

They listed five common reasons that public servants are often bored in meetings. You may recognise some of these from your meetings at Parliament: too long, no clear purpose, no visuals to focus them, no clear outcome, or (my favourite) someone invited that blowhard colleague that just loves to let everybody know how much they've accomplished and all their great ideas, blah, blah, blah.... These delights are the rare people that really *enjoy* going to meetings – so you probably should avoid inviting them to yours....

While we all live in hope that the Higher-ups will one day wise up and scrub our calendars of these time-sucking irrelevancies, that is not happening any day soon. Problem solving is right up there in the 'skill set' requirements in job descriptions when you apply for roles in the Hooseland Public Service, so let's see what 'problem solving' meetings could look like.

First – draw up an agenda – and then rip that up and try and narrow the scope (better a series of shorter meetings with a clear purpose than a long meeting that drags on....). Second – maybe try only inviting *truly* necessary people, the whole meat-in-the-room thing is so 90s, third – make sure everyone attending has the relevant information they need (they never read it, so pick people at random to publicly shame them for this), fourth – don't let motormouth hijack the conversation, and try to keep everyone to the point, sigh, yes I know it is treating them like children, but if the cap fits.... Finally, at the end of all this make sure someone has captured and distilled meeting outcomes into key, actionable points (with people's names highlighted against these actions, a bit of passive aggressiveness ensures they can't wriggle out).

On the bright side, even if you find yourself completely stuck in a pointless and soul sucking meeting there is always something you can do to pass the time, even if your hawk-eyed Higher-up is watching, they cannot police your thoughts. You can think about what your answer will be to the 'where do you see yourself in five years' question at your next job interview or fantasise about how you will resign if you win the lottery. Personally, I find mentally updating my bucket list helps (possibly because it reminds you that one day you will be dead and not have to attend another meeting...).

If you are a good Samaritan and want to alleviate the boredom of your colleagues use one of your empty anxiety medication pill bottles (don't be pretending you don't have one...) and fill it with white Tic Tacs. Place the bottle on the table beside a glass of water and keep taking small handfuls of the pills at a time. However, do be prepared for some kind of a weird intervention meeting at a later date if you decide on that route....

If I ran the world like you do, I would summon the worst rubbish meeting offenders to a meeting and make them watch John Cleese's 1976 classic "Meetings Bloody Meetings". It is timeless – just as relevant today as it was back then – and should be compulsory watching for all Hooseland public servants (and dare I say Ministers...?).

Yours in service to the public,

Amber Guette

Amber Guette (she/her)

Better Together

Dear Minister

I have been thinking about how well the coalition Government you put together is working so far, and of course the public *really* love it when the Government can get together with the Opposition on matters that do not need politics to be played over them, like for example children's welfare and climate change, to establish cross party agreements. It is a joy to see such cooperation!

As is always the case my mind then turned to our public service and how we could learn from that. Sadly, many words have been spoken about trying to fix the impermeable 'silos' in the Hooseland Public Service, so far to no avail. For us to be the innovators we need to be, we have to be trusted more to work with you in the best interests of the public. But before that can happen, our public service needs to learn to work with and trust *each other*. We are a formidable resource and if we could harness the power of a joined up public service, I doubt there is much we could not achieve.

A lack of trust between different departments (or let's be honest, even teams within those departments and individuals within those teams...) just leads to more bureaucracy and obstructs all of us in implementing the Government's policies to the best of our ability. Surely the wicked problems facing us in Hooseland demand unfettered cooperation?

Look, if even a tiny nation like New Zealand, with a population of just over 5 million, can see that the future of good public service lies in breaking down silos why can't we?

Unlike us, they *know* they need to change, because like us, their agencies were actively prevented from collaborating thanks to outdated rules about data-sharing, budget management and staffing. They understand that to deliver better outcomes for their public they needed to operate *across* the system, not just *down* the vertical silos. So, my challenge to our public service is that if they can do it, imagine what Hooseland, with a population of over 42 million can achieve with our budgets? What a win for Hooselanders that would be!

What we urgently need is a proper whole-of-government approach to working collaboratively with public servants in other departments to integrate the 'what' with the 'how', to achieve more efficient and effective implementation of Government policies. Do you realise we actually compete *against* each other to hire the same staff? Good luck to the smaller departments with meagre budgets that cannot offer the wages and conditions of the larger ones when it comes to attracting the best staff.

That may be the only area where we are all after the same thing because we certainly don't use the same IT systems, or terminology which makes information sharing and movement of staff between departments and collaboration in general unnecessarily cumbersome.

This lack of collaboration also makes everything more expensive for the Hooseland public – we are missing out on the buying power of a whole-of-government contract with providers in many cases.

The complex societal problems facing Hooseland such as the disadvantage of our indigenous peoples, climate change, and spiralling homelessness all need to be addressed at the community, family or even individual level, and this urgently requires collaboration between departments that are currently being run as vertically siloed hierarchies, with little or no incentive to change.

If you need further convincing it may be helpful to know that the Hooseland Whole of Government Advisory Group supports the need for our public service to be more collaborative, innovative, risk tolerant and accepting of the failure that can come from experimentation, so that we can learn and improve. The report also points out that far too often the overly complex processes required for information sharing in the Hooseland Public Service get in the way of change.

One of the biggest challenges in collaborating is the competition for budget. Why, oh why, can we not just set up a separate budget for collaborative work, and end the insanity of trying to make things work using several departments budgets? Truth be told, departments have to fight hard to get their budgets in these difficult times, and so feel pressure to deliver the agreed specific goals of their already tightly constrained budget, making it so much harder for them to take the risk of co-resourcing a collaborative project.

Public servants faced with collaboration with other departments too often end up having to fight their corner on who should contribute what to the bucket of money needed to do the work.

Trying to establish a multi-departmental team can feel risky when you are already under enormous pressure, and if the Higher-ups of the people doing the collaborative work don't value it, or see it as taking away their precious resources, they can make life *very difficult* for the poor public servant tasked with running the collaboration. Unfortunately, a lot of our public servants are living this reality every day.

If you want to improve collaboration to deliver the many benefits for the public, then it is critical to establish a separate budget and a strong public service-oriented team culture that supports, encourages and rewards openness between departments.

You also cannot just throw the extra work at public servants that are already drowning in a barrage of 'urgent' requests, torrents of email and just expect them to work longer and longer hours. If the new work means they can no longer do their day job, then you have a resourcing issue, and that has to be factored in when looking at budgets for collaborative work.

Transformation of the public service is often perceived as a challenge. By its very nature, it is often bound up in a complex, outdated, bureaucratic set of rules and regulations, many of which will have been in place for decades, carried out by people who have been in the roles for decades. However, regardless of how large a challenge it is, it is still a challenge that *must* be addressed.

As the Chair of the Hooseland Whole of Government Advisory Group noted, it's easy to *say* that public service silos need to be broken down, but it should be pointed out that this has been the way of the Hooseland Public Service ever since Lord Meldrum Hoose established the first Hooseland Government 323 years ago, so it will take real political will to make these changes.

These silos are not just a waste of resources, they are killers of innovation, and block our ability as public servants to deal with complex problems. I say congratulations to the Higher-ups and teams who are able to successfully establish a unified, cross departmental collaboration with a common goal. We probably need to look more closely at the ones that work so we can better understand how the various parts have come together as a whole.

One of the key elements I have seen in groups that have effectively eliminated their silos is how their motivation was handled. What really defined them as successful for me was the ability of their Higher-ups to identify what motivated *each of the groups* involved, and engage them on that basis, motivation is seriously not a one size fits all kind of gig. They really knew how to stamp out the (in my opinion often infuriating) 'but it's not my job' attitude some public servants sadly seem to have.

Once you have successfully built a cross departmental team, with its own budget, a common goal (even if for rather different motivations) with public servants that feel empowered and supported, it can start to get very exciting, and a pride in the work they are doing can gain momentum and fuel their productivity! And yet we still seem to expect behaviours to just change, because we have forced public servants to work together without addressing any of the issues above.

The exchange of knowledge that the collaboration brings to the departments involved will be absolutely priceless. We know that breaking down silos is not an easy task for any department, however, doing the work needed for this to be done successfully will be a real boost to the motivation of public servants and ultimately, the overall well-being of the departments involved.

Finally, I often hear people say, "oh none of that will ever happen until we get better leadership". Perhaps we should turn that around? Every public servant is a leader in some way, and so we all need to take responsibility – not just sit back and wait until the 'leadership changes'.

Yours in service to the public,

Amber Guette

Amber Guette (she/her)

Everybody's Got to Learn Sometime

Dear Minister

Do Ministers have a union? I guess not, so I suppose you only have your Party Whip to raise issues with. I belong to the Public Service Alliance of Hooseland because I believe that greater good can be achieved if we act as a collective (old fashioned in today's 'me, me, me' world I know).

My expectations of our union may be a wee bit too high though, as I have had a couple of 'run ins' with them, firstly when I asked them at a conference why they had never done any research into the long-term effect of whistleblowing on a public servant's career in Hooseland, and more recently, on why they are not negotiating harder on the need for better professional development for Hooseland's public servants.

It beggars belief why we do not invest more in training new entrants to the Hooseland Public Service and develop them to ensure they stay. They need to know they are valued and with support can continue to add value to our work. Sure, we have multiple small training opportunities on how to use this or that software or process, but not *real* professional development, like certification or degree level courses to develop our career paths with.

The amount of people who become Higher-ups in the Hooseland Public Service that have zero skills or training in management still amazes me. Quite often they don't even *want* to be a Higher-up, but that is the only progression left for them and they have been in the department so long it is expected of them.

I saw a rather mind-blowing thread in the Hooseland Public Service Reddit feed last week where a Higher-up was lamenting that they ever accepted the role of manager – they hated it. They had read the books on how to be a good Higher-up, done the basic online leadership courses the department provided, but they wanted out because they did not feel like they were any *good* at it and they were miserable.

Well, the reaction they got was quite overwhelmingly a list of responses literally *begging* them to stay! Consensus seemed to be that the fact that they cared enough to even consider that they were a crap Higher-up meant that they were likely light years ahead of the ones that did not care. One even said if they were not deliberately *awful* to their team, they had a moral obligation to stay and protect them from the next one who most certainly would be. Yikes.

The research on professional development is clear that when it has clear goals, is relevant to the job, provides meaningful rewards (and results are reflected in development plans and remuneration rounds), it results in improved job experiences and organisational performance. Public servants who pursue professional development in their careers tend to have higher productivity and job satisfaction. What's not to like? Sounds like a good investment in the service of the public to me.

On the flip side of that is what we often see in reality – HR and Higher-ups failing to set clear goals, give relevant feedback, get staff to participate in the process, reward good performance and – just as importantly – address poor performance. I have said it before, but it bears repeating that the fastest thing you can do to demoralise a great employee is to tolerate a poor one. If there are no consequences for poor performance, why should anyone strive for excellence?

Indeed, it is well known fact in the Hooseland Public Service that some extremely mediocre, if not just plain awful, individuals seem to keep making their way up the ladder despite the fact that they are known to be suffering from some of the less savoury 'bureaupathologies' outlined in my Human Centipede letter.

Perhaps the most interesting learning a public servant gets is the 'on-job' learning. I don't just mean the kind, very patient colleague sitting next to you that calmly walks you through the pivot table function on a spreadsheet for the 4th time. I include here the 'monkey see monkey do' method of learning. Employees need to be convinced that their TOTP is committed to serving the public, and not just a self-interested careerist who acts like a sycophant, constantly putting their Minister's wants ahead of the public needs, as they slime their way towards a knighthood.

A recent survey in the Hooseland Clarion showed that public servants rate their workplace experience fourteen points lower than the overall private sector average (59% versus 73% positive). The biggest reason behind this discrepancy is the public service has lagged behind on investment in innovative, better tools for employees, so consequently, their interactions are difficult and more fragmented.

To give you a real-world example at CHAOS it can take nearly 30 minutes every morning getting your laptop set up because it is an artifact from 2013 and likes to act its age. On top of that we have to do a work around in order to get it to Bluetooth to the monitors because it is not compatible with the docking station. Add to this the Olympic sport that is "hot-desking" (not as exotic as it sounds – more like a game of musical chairs, but with desks, other people's crumbs and coffee stains and *way* more annoying) so it is never the same monitors on consecutive days. Now here's the fun bit – you have to register the Bluetooth connection with each monitor you use separately – and in order to link to that monitor you need to be within a 2-metre distance of it. And the desks either side of you and the three in the row opposite you are less than 2 metres away, so it becomes a game of Russian roulette as to which monitor the laptop will decide to mate with, leaving you wondering why you cannot see your login screen only to find it is showing up two desks down....

Hooseland's government departments also could benefit from creating opportunities for mentoring. There is a lot to be said for providing the opportunity for mentoring for new and not so new public servants. I say not so new because mentoring should never be one way traffic – just as older public servants have skills and knowledge to share – so do our newly minted ones. You could have a skills bank on your intranet – where skills in handling meetings or briefing ministers could be traded for technical skills or tips on how to utilise social media in your engagement with the public.

Speaking of social media, don't get me started on connectivity in the office – our Teams meetings are more like some kind of modern day seance, what with the ghosting, people disappearing or freezing mid-sentence (can be hard to tell with the quieter ones if they have frozen or are just trying to be really inconspicuous so no one asks them a question) the cries of "I think someone wants to join us", "Curtis are you there – we can hear you, but we cannot see you – can you see us!??? Whole portions of conversations just lost to the ether along with the reason for the meeting itself.

Hooseland's public servants don't want the top-of-the-line latest gear, they just need their work tools and technology to be at least reliable and not a struggle to use. Investing in the right equipment means that public servants can get on with the job they are there to do for our public. When public servants feel connected, they are more satisfied, engaged, and productive. Even more so as younger generations join the public service, providing working technology is crucial to attracting, developing, and retaining talent.

Investing in education and technology for the Hooseland Public Service will provide a workforce that is current, technically astute and fit to serve our public. More of the monkey see monkey do learning and less monkeying around trying to get a signal! I hope you have learnt something new today Minister.

Yours in service to the public,

Amber Guette (she/her)

Tubthumping
(I Get Knocked Down)

Dear Minister

I need to vent – I am fuming!! I was walking home from work on Monday, and I met on old colleague a couple of blocks from work. It was starting to get dark (please thank your team for me for that late, last minute urgent request BTW) and it took me a while to realise he had a band-aid on his head. I pointed it out and joked saying, I hoped the other person was in worse shape. He looked pretty sheepish and told me it was his Higher-up that had done it! Apparently, they lost the plot over a reported leak to the media and threw the stapler on their desk at him (his team was pointed out as a possible source but trust me he is the last person to do something like that, a professional through and through – clearly unlike his Higher-up!).

I was hoping to write about something more positive this month until this happened, but now it is time we talked about the public service's biggest problem. Bullying.

Bullying in the Hooseland Public Service is not just a matter of isolated incidents, it is a chronic illness, and it is just not acceptable, but it happens far too often.

Okay, this really pushes my buttons, but I am going to keep this as calm as I can. It is probably a good idea to start with what bullying is and what is generally not considered bullying. Bullying is unsolicited, vindictive, cruel, malicious, or humiliating attempts to undermine an individual, or group. These are generally persistently negative attacks on personal and professional performance and are usually unpredictable, irrational and often unseen. Bullying normally consists of repeated behaviour.

Bullying is not legitimate or constructive advice (hard as that can be to hear sometimes), reasonable action by Higher-ups, or reasonable comments between public servants. Recent investigations by the Hooseland Clarion have thrust cases of bullying and harassment within our public service into the spotlight.

Since publishing their series of stories on this, they have had a ton of feedback from public servants, thanking them and backing up their research. Negative workplace behaviour has been a serious problem within Hooseland government departments for years, and it isn't going away on its own.

On the back of the Clarion's investigation, government departments have even admitted staff are not reporting bullying and harassment, with bad behaviour much more common than official numbers show. Some departments say their figures are artificially low because they are aware people are often too frightened to report it for fear of ruining their career prospects.

In many cases, the Hooseland Public Service has only just started reporting bullying in the past couple of years, and only because of work done by media like the Clarion. This is our dirty little secret in the public service, and it needs to see the light of day before anything will change.

Have I witnessed it myself? You betcha – here is a classic example from the second department I worked in, this particular TOTP was often described as being volatile at meetings, with public servants not knowing when the next 'explosion' would be, I was told after leaving by one of his direct reports that they actually took sedatives prior to meetings with him, as they were his favourite target for what almost seemed to be a sport for him, in bullying and shaming them in 'leadersheep' team meetings.

This particular instance was with a brand-new graduate public servant, starting work on their first day in the TOTP's office. They were asked by the TOTP to take the office credit card and get a list of office supplies for his office that were not provided by the Ministry. I heard him say to the newbie as she was leaving that he rather liked purple ink pens.

On returning with the requested items, that happened to include two purple ink ballpoint pens, she set about putting the items away in his office. As she was leaving, I heard him call her back into his office in a rather gruff manner. I waited nervously for her to return to her desk as this TOTP was known for being a particularly mean individual, and when she eventually came back, she was visibly upset. I grabbed her coat and took her out of the building for a coffee and she told me that the TOTP had berated her for getting the purple ink ballpoint pens – stating that the two statements ("get the list of office supplies" and "purple ink ballpoints are my favourites" were *not* in any way connected (even though ballpoint pens of an unstated colour were on the list) – and that she had made an assumption. It was a *test* and she had failed.... I ask you, what kind of *twisted* sociopath, in any way thinks that this is an okay way to treat someone? How do you think that coloured that young woman's view of the Hooseland Public Service?

What was *wrong* with that TOTP?? They just seemed to want to extinguish the spirit and the excitement of this young person, who clearly walked into the office that morning very happy to be there. Were they jealous of her zest for life!? I can't even begin to understand their motivation... but I saw the light go out in her eyes and she continued working there, but as a shadow of her former self.

If leaders in our public service can act like that how on earth do they expect the rest of public service to behave? What leaders do matters! Every Hooseland public servant deserves to work in a safe and inclusive workplace, where people treat one another with respect.

Despite public servant surveys across all areas of the public service making it clear that this is an endemic problem, it is all too often swept under the mat, and therefore never fully addressed.

We need to establish an independent entity (my preference is for an Ombudsman for Public Servants) to enable public servants to report bullying and other unacceptable behaviour. No public servant could ever feel safe taking up such matters within their own departments for fear of reprisals if they reported it. And anyone reported and found to be guilty of that type of behaviour should be seen to be sanctioned for it (have not seen that happen yet!), not be promoted (have seen that), and then maybe behaviour will finally change if others can see there are consequences for this shameful behaviour.

According to the Clarion, the most frequently reported forms of bullying are verbal abuse, derogatory remarks, being ignored, or being yelled at. Sometimes it can be something as insidious as withholding information that person needs to do their work, therefore setting them up to fail, or even blatantly sabotaging their work. The third most common form is the unfair application of work policies or rules and blocking access to leave or training. And we are not talking about a handful of people here, *75 percent* of the Hooseland Public Service have reported seeing harassment or bullying in their workplace but did not report their experiences because they did not believe any action would be taken, or that they would suffer consequences for speaking out.

We need people to feel they can speak up, safe in the knowledge that they will be taken seriously, and that there *will* be consequences for the perpetrator. I was once told by a colleague that had been the victim of inappropriate comments and touching, that they had finally summoned the courage to report this behaviour to HR, only to have the Higher-up not just remain in the public service, but to actually get *promoted*.

It seems that a lot of lip service is paid to 'values', 'ethics' and 'Codes of Conduct' in the Hooseland Public Service – perhaps we need to move beyond these department mandated documents and as public servants come up with a Public Servants Manifesto for *all* public servants that states beyond any doubt the behaviour we expect in the workplace? Watch this space...

Yours in service to the public,

Amber Guette (she/her)

Waiting For the Great Leap Forwards

Dear Minister

I hope you had a great Guy Fawkes — actually, that is a funny thought isn't it, politicians celebrating someone who was intent on blowing them all up? On the topic of blowing things up there is something I have been meaning to talk to you about. I have been hearing whispers in the office kitchen about yet another restructure here at CHAOS (we are still trying to recover from the last one less than 18 months ago!), I am hoping I am not too late in alerting you to the realities of what this means for public servants. You see if bullying is the public service's chronic illness, then restructures are our cancer.

We all knew it was bad news when Cruella (whose track record has already been ascertained) started to meet with the head of HR on a regular basis. Added to this, any request made to replace staff that were leaving (normally a pretty straight forward affair, despite Paula in HR's best efforts...) has been met with a blanket "put that on hold until further notice". So many red flags we started to think we were at the circus....

I know you are *relatively* new to government, but you should know that restructures happen so often that any change of leadership in the Hooseland Public Service tends to be the death knell for stability. Yet another distraction from our work serving the public and meeting your election promises. The chilling effect restructures have on morale is just awful, and it completely stuffs our ability to retain any staff quick enough to see the writing on the wall. These are the very insightful people we need to keep, but of course being smart they will jump ship way before any major announcements are made.

Watching HR clumsily conduct a 'consultation' with the department on the last restructure draft document (of course it had been developed in complete isolation from those affected) was very painful. Timeframes were far too short for real discussion, and the 'consensus' decision making that was proclaimed to be the goal of it. It was very clear to everyone, that despite the high quality of the response to the document, none of their feedback was taken in for the final document. What a major waste of their time and the public's hard earned tax dollars.

Don't get me wrong, done well and for the right reasons I think a thoughtful restructure can really improve the performance of a department and even make it a more exciting and vibrant place to work. But sadly, that type of restructure is few and far between. Did you know that since CHAOS was established 28 years ago, we have had 19 restructures – 19! The Hooseland Public Service's TOTP's are responsible over the years for more restructuring than the *entire Commonwealth nations put together.* Has this become a competition!? Or are we living in an extended series of The Apprentice? This is madness, surely any meaningful change takes years to bed-in and bear fruit. Of course, at this point the TOTP that inflicted the change will have earned a place high up the ladder as a reward for this behaviour, *or* the Government will change and either way it becomes here we go again....

I imagine that when you get enough critical mass on these things, they become self-perpetuating, as other TOTP's feel the pressure to look like they are 'innovative' and have 'vision' too. Or worse, the restructure results in a failure to launch any improvements, and internal blame and recrimination lead to the next restructure! I am surely no expert, but the optics from here are not great.

Look, I accept that change is the one constant in life, and I had even brought a poster from home to try and jolly the team along stating, "It is not the strongest of the species that survives, nor the most intelligent. It is the one most adaptable to change". Of course, this has since had to be taken down, as personal items at work were banned under the most recent restructure....

They often try to justify a restructure as a 'cost cutting' exercise, but the real cost to the public is much higher than any supposed 'savings'. Firstly, the recruitment freeze that happens while the usually six months to one year restructure process is undertaken, often requires more pricey temps and contractors to plug the gaps, not to mention the intellectual capital that is lost when the people with knowledge and expertise walk out the door. And all those expensive consultants that are brought in to rearrange the deck chairs.... Some people just leave because they can't *bear* another restructuring, or don't want to work under the new regime.

And then, once all the talent has walked out the door you are left with all the 'deadwood' that have been there so long it would cost way too much to make them redundant, so they become part of the next stage in the restructure – the dreaded internal recruitment process.... This is the really fun part, where an extraordinary amount of time is used in preparing applications, going for interviews, convening panels, working out who is eligible and who is not. It is like an extended episode of that dodgy sitcom, The Bachelorette, watching the rivalries and petty jealousies as colleague duke it out for the 'Assistant Head of Stationary Supplies' role in the department. If indeed, as it is often touted, the aim of a restructure is to improve efficiencies, then history shows that this is far from being the outcome.

You know the definition of madness is doing the same thing over and over and expecting a different result. I recommend that a bit more thought be put into this particular kind of madness. There are many other ways of achieving greatness of reputation (which is what I gather these TOTPs are trying to achieve) then staging a restructure. Some of these TOTPs have about as much imagination as the military in right wing developing countries (Coup anyone?).

There are plenty of better alternatives to restructuring. For example, they may want to consider *directly* managing any staff performance issues, or exploring incremental adjustments to structure or functions? How about becoming the poster child for breaking down silos and setting up cross-agency working groups rather than new organisations? I don't want to be *too* radical, but have they ever thought of asking public servants how *they* think improvements could be made?? As the outcome of restructuring often means that the few people left are expected to carry out the 'more with less' edicts, and given the effect the process has on morale, you would think *some* attempt would be made to make the process less traumatic If not on economic, then at least on humanitarian grounds?

The most depressing bit is that I have seen restructures where if they bothered looking at just *one* report on global best practice, they would have known that it was never going to work.... How are we ever going to learn from our own mistakes if we can't even be bothered to learn from others?

Lots of television metaphors in this letter isn't there? So, to continue with that theme, if there is indeed going to be yet another restructure then please, Beam me up Scotty....

Yours in service to the public,

Amber Guette (she/her)

Bloody Well Right

Dear Minister

The middle of winter and the CHAOS Department's 'motivational' screensaver has changed to suit the weather, providing us with lots of lovely snowy nature scenes. Not sure what they think they are supposed to be motivating us to do? Flee from our fluorescent tube lit boxes to the wonders of nature? They may do better giving us images of homeless people or data on the rising cost of living rates to keep us peddling hard on our hamster wheels. Speaking of motivation, I can share with you one of the worst things you can do for the motivation of public servants – muzzle us.

And I do not just mean in terms of what we say in public, this can even be a problem in the workplace. Have you ever been in a meeting, raising a legitimate, if controversial, topic only to have your Higher-up say, 'Let's offline that discussion'? Of course, the point being that they hope you will forget and that you and your colleagues will learn not to raise uncomfortable subject matters anymore. While I agree that if it is deployed genuinely, for example when things are getting too much in the weeds and derailing the purpose of the meeting, then it serves a purpose. But if it is used too often it can have a chilling effect on public servants' ability to raise controversial topics.

Under the previous Hooseland Government changes were made to the guidelines on how public servants should use social media. The guidelines state that outside of their work as a public servant, (expressing in their private capacity, as a tax paying Hooselander in their own free time) *any* disagreement with a government policy, or even 'liking' a negative social media post could put Hooseland public servants in hot water. This feels a lot like overt politicisation of the public service. I note that although we are well into the second term of the new Government those guidelines have not been modified in any way, so perhaps it has just slipped under the radar?

Meanwhile, if you are thinking that *you* would *never* seek to muzzle public servants, bear in mind that the lack of tenure for the TOTP's more than likely makes them inclined to encourage compliance with the Government of the day, thus again inadvertently politicising the public service.

Clearly individual public servants must be entitled to have their own political views just like any other Hooselander. The idea of us being 'political eunuchs' is crazy and undemocratic, the secret of course is balance. Spending many years as a public servant under a Government I did not vote for was never a conflict for me, as my role was to serve the public – and they had chosen the Government. This is still one of the best arguments I can think of for keeping public service from becoming politicised, Governments may come and go like the tides on a sea of public opinion, while we are like the land – still there for the long-haul, if a bit eroded by the winds of change.

Why is it okay to praise the Government, but not to disagree with it? Doesn't this make a mockery of the point of the guidelines – to increase public servant's impartiality. These social media guidelines are designed to silence public servants and have a chilling effect on the ability of public servants to be part of a democratic Hooseland.

I should add that I speak from personal experience. A

couple of years ago I shared the Twitter post created by the Hooseland First Nations #ask_the_question_Hooseland from my private Twitter account AmberGuette@Hooseland. The next week when I went to work, I was called in to my Higher-up's office to explain why I was publicly supporting anti-government social media? (Apparently a colleague who followed me on Twitter had 'accidentally' mentioned it in front of them). I replied that I did it because I fully agreed with the Hooseland First Nations that we should be asking 'Hooseland', as it had clearly been stolen from the original occupants and colonised by an Englishman who had been told to bugger off by his own inbred aristocratic family because of his opium habit. I added that as a taxpaying citizen of Hooseland I had every right to voice my support. My punishment? I was told I could no longer run the CHAOS Social Club.... I replied that was a reward, not a punishment, and good luck finding anyone else willing to take on the herculean task of getting the IOU's paid back by the department's borderline alcoholic staff....

If the Government and the TOTP's *really* don't want public servants feeling like they have to vent publicly, then at the very least perhaps they should consider encouraging internal integrity systems that not only allow, but actively encourage public servants to raise concerns within their departments? I also think reinstating the Hooseland Public Service Employee Survey would go some way to giving public servants a voice. It was quietly replaced six years ago with a new survey that is just brimming with patsy questions designed to illicit the types of responses the TOTP deem acceptable.

Sure, the old survey may have had some embarrassing news for them from time to time, such as stats that suggested that while 91% of TOTP rated their performance as high, only

23% of public servants gave them the same rating (and FYI that 23% just about fits with the level of nepotism currently in the Hooseland Public Service). Despite those kinds of inconveniences, it was valuable in terms of getting honest feedback on the health of the Hooseland Public Service and held management to account.

From a public interest perspective, Hooselanders pay our wages – do they not therefore deserve to have our informed contribution to political debate? As long as public servants are doing this in our own time, and we do not identify ourselves as public servants, shouldn't we have the same rights to express our opinions?

It of course goes without saying that public servants cannot reveal classified information, or information that has not been publicly released, or that they are privy to only in the course of their duties. The right to individual opinions and political involvement does *not* get in the way of public servants carrying out their responsibilities to implement the policies of the Government of the day to the best of their abilities.

It is not just Hooseland public servants that can be made to suffer from attempts to silence their voices publicly, we also inflict 'gagging clauses' (clauses in contracts that prevent organisations from speaking out on matters that do not align with government) on Hooseland civil society organisations for the social services they provide for us. The upshot of this being that those at the coalface with the best information are stopped from sharing that with the media or the public. Organisations that go against this may even lose their funding. I can only imagine the moral quandary this puts them in.

I recently came across a very funny chat room that just consisted of unidentifiable public servants venting by typing their biggest irritants in all caps, these irritants all looked pretty familiar, and it seemed to give them some sense of relief, but no one who really needed to hear that got to hear it, it just stayed in their own very frustrated echo chamber – what a waste of free and frank information.

#ask_the_question_Hooseland!

Yours in service to the public,

Amber Guette (she/her)

Mercy, Mercy Me

Dear Minister

What keeps you up at night? Or do you sleep soundly? I will tell you what currently keeps *me* up at night – the sudden uptick in the sport of public servant blaming! I did not expect this from your Government, but it feels like every other week one or another of your colleagues is naming and shaming a public servant in the media. Call me old fashioned, but it was always an unwritten rule in Hooseland politics that Ministers take the blame if things go wrong as they have the right of reply. Your side of the bargain gets to make the final decision on policy, so the outcomes sit squarely with you.

In my experience, politicians either complain about the public service when they are in opposition (calling us lackeys or similar) or when they are starting to lose in the polls and start blaming public officials for their downfall. It is a cowardly move as they know full well that there is very little we can do about it. We serve the Government of the day and have no public 'right of reply'.

This feeds right into the hands of the tabloids who have always been selling the message that the public service is lazy, wasteful, complacent, and dedicated to frustrating the will of politicians. That has *never* been true, but that hasn't stopped it being their mantra for decades.

The convention that public servants do not speak in public is partly to blame for this. There are no votes to be won by defending the value of public servants, and the more conservative elements of the public have an ideological bias against the whole notion of public service, so the public service is effectively defenceless against media attacks. There used to be something special about getting into the Hooseland Public Service, a sense of pride that you were there to make a difference for the public, but that train is leaving the station. We need to fix that Minister.

Sure, the public service is far from faultless and there can be a tendency to over complicate things. I am the first to admit that risk averseness and paperwork slow things down, and that middle management can cause blockages or that we are unnecessarily siloed and need to work together without being forced to.

I think what I'm saying is that a lot of the blaming of the public service does have a bit of truth to it. Pretending this isn't the case is not helpful. However, it does not take much reflection to work out why the public service has those behaviours. Most stem from risk averseness bought on by fear of Government retaliation if something goes wrong – so a self-perpetuating cycle it seems.

Perhaps things would be immeasurably better if people actually had an understanding of what we do, why we do it, and how vital these things are to the public. I'm just not sure how we get there.

Maybe the only way to change this is if public servants all went on strike en masse and brought the whole system down so that Hooselanders see how much we do every day to keep this country going and how little the people in power do in terms of the day-to-day stuff. We need to remain proud of being public servants.

For all the problems in Hooseland right now (and there are many), we have peace, relative stability, running water, the lights are on, schools are decent, and people may have to wait for a long time to get an appointment, but we have a world-class health system that is free. That's because of public servants. We keep the country going despite the vagaries of changing Governments.

I am going to share with you some of the good things public servants do – all the things we cannot go to the media and share, all the reasons we keep coming into work to serve the Hooseland public. I am hoping you will have the courage to remind your colleagues that along with the Code of Conduct for the public service there is an unwritten code of conduct that they are breaking.

I asked my fellow public servants what they had done in their daily work that gave them pride, what they had done to protect and deflect the constant messaging in the media that public servants are lazy, wasteful and complacent. Here are their words:

- "For me it's when I have been able to help the public on an individual level. I have had people turn up stressed out having just realised their passport would not be valid by the end of their travel, on the day of their flight. Processing their application and printing their new passport there and then and handing it to them so they didn't miss their flight was a very happy moment."
- "I got 42 young people into paid employment and training in a 48-hour period some time in 2018/2019. The methods I used were cascaded up the channels and helped contribute to 100,000 young people moving into employment. That was a good week at work."
- "Finding a way to make our websites information more accessible to parts of the community that we had inadvertently locked out by ensuring translation, text-to-speak functions and plain English etc, were utilised."

- "Helping a 16-year-old abuse victim get the benefit they were entitled to and finding them a safe place to sleep."
- "We helped ensure that schools in less well-off areas were warm and dry and got engaged with local community groups to ensure the kids had a warm lunch each day."
- "Stopping the abuse of elderly dementia sufferers by family members."
- "Making sure an abused 61-year-old chap with severe autism was able to have a bloody good birthday party before he died. But I forgot, public servants are just lazy bureaucrats that never achieve anything, right?"
- "My proudest day was when we stopped crooked solicitors from taking advantage of people with learning difficulties."
- "Our work allowed an extra 10,000 international students to get a post-study work visa as I noticed a problem before anyone else and got a policy change/ fix underway before the sector noticed the issue. Amazing seeing the stats!"
- "I'm proud of some of the Hooseland legislation I've worked on. Banning adults from smoking in cars when children are present is one that I can happily point to."
- "Our team helps settle refugees into Hooseland, it is an honour to see our country through their eyes and realise how lucky we are and how much we have to gain by sharing, people take what we have here for granted, I think. It is easy to complain."
- "We built over 11,000 rent-to-buy homes for low-income families who could never afford a home through conventional means – the looks on their faces when they step over the threshold, and we hand them the keys always puts a skip in my step."
- "My job might seem boring to some, I work in an office

all day with paperwork on APFIA requests, but I take pride in ensuring our responses are transparent and fulsome with helpful context, and, where it can be, in plain English that does not talk down to the requester. I feel like I am one of the guards of democracy – I love my job."

- "I work in a call centre, and sometimes we get elderly callers, and you can tell the conversation is the only contact they have had with another person all week, so I take my time with them and engage in banter and try to get a chuckle out of them. It helps make dealing with the angry ones more bearable."

My advice to my fellow public servants would be that they are the only one who truly knows what they do to add to the good in this world. If they keep people at the centre of everything they do, and refuse to let process, officiousness or self-promotion become their mantra then they can still have a very rewarding career as a public servant in Hooseland. If they don't wait for these opportunities to make a difference to come their way, but make them happen, they will see how much more rewarding their work can be.

They need to be reminded that sometimes when serving the public, they will get abused. None of that is about them (but it is hard not to take it personally). The people they are talking to are not angry at them. They may be yelling at them and calling them names, but they are not angry at them. They are angry at themselves, their situation, the ex-husband who's gambling got them in this mess in the first place that lost their house, and more, and any combination of them. What does that mean? It's not *their* fault or responsibility. We need to build in peer support with other public servants. No one is alone (but we often think we are). But we must also remember that every day we get up and choose to serve the Hooseland public with heart we are choosing to do the better thing.

Yours in service to the public,

Amber Guette (she/her)

The Otherside

Dear Minister

Start of spring this weekend! Hooseland's winter has been very hard, and we have had lots of highly contagious coughs and colds going around so I have decided that I am going to warm you up with some ideas on how we can improve empathy levels both within the public service and for the public, because empathy is also highly contagious.

Sometimes it must feel like it is all bad news from me, but that is only because I really want the best for our public servants, and through them the public. And yes – it really is sometimes just a *few bad apples* that spoil the barrel, but spoil it they do, as they have the power to take the oxygen out of the room and create a toxic atmosphere that the rest of us have to somehow survive.

Of course, we do not want to just survive, we want to *thrive* and shift the needle further towards all the good things we are and can be in the Hooseland Public Service. What I think may be missing is empathy, and if there is no empathy for public servants how can they be expected to show that to the public?

I met with a wonderful person last week who was new to the public service and had been put in a Team Leader role in one of our busy teams here at CHAOS. They asked if we could go for a coffee and a chat, as they needed to try and make sense of the environment they had found themselves in, I agreed.

Firstly, I would like to say how pleased I am that they came to work in the Hooseland Public Service. They exemplified compassion, empathy and quiet strength. We sat down, and they proceeded to tell me that in their one-on-ones with their new team members, they had been shocked to have about a third of them break down crying at the stress and workload they were under, and some told him they were going to be leaving very soon, as they just could not take it anymore.

This Team Leader, as you can imagine, was mortified. They expressed genuine concern for their team members and showed compassion for their situation. They listened and told them they were here now, and that things were going to change.

This newly minted public servant explained to me that in their previous role in the private sector it was understood that at the end of the day, the only thing that really mattered was the people, because if they were not okay how could anything else be? I nearly wept because *this person got it*. People *are* the only thing that matter – and it seems that is rarely understood by many of the Higher-ups in the Hooseland Public Service.

Lots of studies show that empathy is a vital skill for public servants, but you would hardly believe that if you looked at the professional development offerings for us. Having a sense of empathy not only makes us better at our jobs, but it helps us feel more engaged and fulfilled in our work as well.

If we are to develop the wise public policymakers and leaders we need in the Hooseland Public Service, we need to include empathy along with integrity as core skills, not just as fluffy nice-to-haves that can be dispensed with if they are not in that particular Higher-ups skill set. The old saying that you measure what you treasure has never been truer when it comes to Key Performance Indicators, adding these soft skills as part of a Higher-up's performance measurements would surely shake things up?

We need to begin by defining what empathy means in the public service. Having empathy means being able to understand what the world looks and feels like from another's point of view. Valuing and building this skill in the public service (as well as our politicians?) will improve how we serve the public and implement public policy. Active empathy offers a way to improve our interactions and behaviours and bring to life the public service values we espouse.

When Hooseland public servants were asked what the most important characteristic of a good public servant is the majority responded with empathy. A similar response was given when asked what the number one quality of a great Higher-up was, this time empathy and integrity were first equal.

Being a public servant is a decent, relatively safe career. But then, so is banking. The reason that public servants work the jobs they do is, above all else, impact. Impact is what makes (nearly) all the frustrations and challenges worthwhile. Above all, public servants are motivated by doing good.

Public servants want to help the public at a local and global level, and that's what makes our work so important. But there is a price that is paid if all the empathy and compassion is one way traffic and is only flowing out from the public servants and not towards them.

Compassion fatigue (yes, it is a thing) is one of the many ways public servants can experience burnout. It can accompany and potentially amplify other mental health issues, and be experienced as insomnia, anxiety or depression.

Increasingly burnout and stress are fuelled by low levels of engagement, increasing workloads with decreasing resources and a lack of compassion from colleagues and Higher-ups. But, despite an increasing number of studies finding multiple positive effects from compassion in the workplace, surprisingly little is being done about it in Hooseland.

So, what should the Higher-ups be doing to fix this? None of this is rocket science, it is pretty much Human Being 101 and should come as a standard practice in Higher-ups, but it seems HR don't make sure people have basic human qualities (as many do not seem to have them themselves) before they let them into the public service, so here goes, the humanity guidelines for a Higher-up:

- Check in with team members regularly on an individual basis, in a private space and connect with them on a human level before getting into the work side of things, show *genuine* interest in their goals and aspirations and life outside work.
- When there is change afoot talk to them about it, seek their input into decisions that affect them – 'nothing done to us without us' is not just for members of the public.
- Leaders need to show their human side; share their failings (this advice will go down like cold sick for some of the Higher-ups but if that is their reaction you have to ask whether they should be in the role in the first place!) and how those experiences made you a stronger, wiser, person.
- Be approachable and listen with an open mind, do *not* be that terrifying boss that throws staplers at people because you are having a bad day.
- Try to understand their perspectives. You don't need to agree with everything they say, but it's important to see their point of view.

- Keep an eye out for burnout. Overworking is a serious issue in the public service, and beyond your team members own mental distress, it can really affect the things that *your* Higher-up will judge *you* on – the team's output, retention and overall morale, etc.
- Focus on understanding how your choices impact your team, and lead by example – if you want to play the martyr by never taking leave, just remember how that can look to others, if you do not show self-care how can you expect them to? Wear sunscreen....

When compassion and empathy become part of the Hooseland Public Service culture it will be contagious, and the (voting!) public will be the immediate beneficiaries, which will lead to more approval for your Government. While every public servant should be equipped and encouraged to do all these things, this behaviour will only thrive when it is supported by the TOTP, it's that good old 'tone at the top' chestnut.

And so, if a public servant is brave enough to report on a colleagues/Higher-up's misconduct then they need to know that they are taken seriously and that there are consequences for that behaviour. They need to see their leaders act decisively and investigate with integrity. There needs to be a clear conclusion with fair sanctions: penalties should be proportionate to the extent of the offence corrected for mitigating and aggravating circumstances.

Given that late dump of snow that is forecast a lot of us will have to work from home due to blocked roads. That will mean the rise and rise of that double edged sword that is the virtual office for a week or two (laundry anyone?). So, for fun, I am signing off with an amusing, but accurate, haiku I saw once to mark the change of work venue.

When working from home
Virtual meetings are now a thing.
No one has pants on.

Yours in service to the public,

Amber Guette

Amber Guette (she/her)

It Isn't Enough

Dear Minister

I mention the weather a lot, don't I? Social conditioning, I guess. My mother did that, you could never call her without getting a running commentary on the weather where she lived and enquiring as to what the weather was doing where you were, or more often, her telling you what the weather was where you were. Apparently, it is a popular pastime in Ireland and the Irish do tend to be weather obsessed, well she certainly was, bless her.

And yet for all my chit chat about the weather I have just realised that the biggest single issue facing the human race has not yet been raised properly in my correspondence – climate change. Now that winter has finally finished here in Hooseland we are all keenly aware that this has been the worst on record. The flooding alone has been horrendous, but add to that the number of black-outs due to crazy low temperatures and let's just say that anyone in Hooseland that is still a climate change denier is seriously living in cloud cuckoo land...

And all the while here we are beavering away on progressing the new Community Health Centres, and it just occurred to me that the focus of this Government seems to just be more ambulance at the bottom of the cliff thinking.

This is a problem that demands innovative future planning, urgent preventative action and long-term mitigations to fend off the worst of the effects for the planet. But what are we doing in Hooseland – tinkering at the edges as the unavoidable reality of how bad the future is looking for the human race (and all the other poor bloody species have to share this planet with us).

The only way I can begin to forgive humanity for this sleep walking to the destruction of our planet is to believe they are overwhelmed/depressed and in denial about it. When it comes to the denial, I think there may be a solution that might just work. It is a bit radical but bear with me.

Unless you are less progressive than I believe you to be, (I hear you do actually inhale...) you will be well aware that in recent years there has been a resurgence in scientific interest on the psychological effects of psychedelic drugs. For example, in recent trials where psilocybin (the magic part of magic mushrooms) was administered to people diagnosed with treatment-resistant depression, they reported significantly positive responses even six months later. Could this be the key to overcoming inaction in the face of the climate crisis?

As well as "resetting" key brain circuitry and enhancing emotional responsiveness, psychedelics increase people's positive feelings of 'connectedness'– to themselves and others, and to the natural world.

Yes, I know that solving the climate crisis requires more than shifts in individual perspective, but desperate times call for desperate measures and the Government's response to climate change, as I have to say I am a bit shocked at the lukewarm attempts so far to address the biggest existential threat we have faced as a nation.

At this stage, the planet is set to exceed and even double the 1.5 degrees temperature threshold in our lifetime. At this rate, even a 99% commitment to tackling climate change is not enough, we need to make every possible effort in order to avoid disaster.

I am well aware my fellow public servants share my concerns (not often we all agree). The Department for the Environment have done some great work on researching what Hooselanders want to see happening on this front. As we are an evidence based and data hungry bunch, let us start with what we know about Hooselanders priorities.

I am not sure how much interest you are taking in your colleague's portfolio in this area, so I am going to share the results, and apologies if I am teaching you to suck eggs and you have already seen them. They do seem *rather* pertinent to your health portfolio.... Okay, so from the survey done in autumn we can confirm that the majority of Hooselanders (those lovely people that voted you in) want the government to play a much larger role in addressing climate change. About two-thirds (66%) of Hooselanders say the government is doing too little to reduce the effects of climate change – a view that's about as widely held this year as it was last autumn, so no improvement there.

And public dissatisfaction with the government's environmental action is not limited just to climate change. There is also wide concern that too little is being done in protecting air and water quality and endangered native wildlife (nobody wants the Big Footed Crowing Senex to go extinct now do they?).

Consistent with Hooselanders concerns over climate and the environment, 81% of Hooselanders agree the priority for the country's energy supply should be developing alternative sources of energy, such as wind and solar; far fewer (19%) give priority to expanding the production of oil, coal and natural gas.

To shift our energy consumption toward renewables, a majority of the public (68%) says government regulations will be necessary to encourage businesses and individuals to rely more on renewable energy; fewer (32%) think the private marketplace will ensure this change in habits. The most popular short-term solution, favoured by 90% of Hooselanders, is to plant about a trillion trees to absorb carbon emissions.

While I can see that *some* change is happening (great that the fleet of Parliament cars are now electric, and very appropriate that parliament's sewage is being reticulated to its drinking water), it is slow and far from ambitious, and there seems to be a painful hangover from the previous Government, on the ability of private interests and the powerful industry lobbying bodies to hamper progress. How can they possibly continue to ignore the fact that we are on the edge of global disaster?!

Given the very clear mandate from the Hooseland public in the above data, the Government is falling short in acting with urgency to uphold the majority will. It feels like Groundhog Day, and once again we are stalling in the face of pressure from profit-driven corporations and fringe stakeholders. Beyond the worrying lack of action on climate change, it would seem that the government is undermining democracy by not taking the will of the majority of Hooselanders seriously enough?

The tinkering at the edges that we are doing is just buying time until we are faced with being beyond the threshold that we can come back from. If policymaking is truly driven by what the public want, then addressing climate change is surely a top priority for the Government? As you well know I am a big fan of the new health clinics for the community, but in order to protect the future health of Hooselanders we need urgent action, or it will just be more ambulances at the bottom of the cliff...

By not undertaking the critical reform required to

prevent and mitigate the worst effects of the climate crisis we are just joining the other wealthy nations (all of us equally responsible for the current levels of emissions...) and turning a blind eye, because we are not as vulnerable as the poorer nations.

Overall, Hooseland has done relatively little to reduce carbon emissions, invest in non-renewable energies, or provide educational programs to support environmentally responsible and sustainable practises. We urgently need to shift our mindset and embrace the idea that investing in environmentally sustainable practises is a lot cheaper and more economic in the long run. And as the 'long run' is the purview of public servants you can probably understand why I am getting a *wee* bit agitated...

You see, even if the world wakes up and makes a serious effort to curb greenhouse gas emissions, some degree of climate change can't be avoided (indeed it is already being felt). And it is putting our people at risk. The extreme events this winter threatened our critical infrastructure.

So, how about instead of all the nice words and policy papers and select committees we actually start *doing* something. The Monty Python Life of Brian 'committee meeting' accurately reflects the current state of climate action in Hooseland). We have all heard the phrase "actions speak louder than words" but in my experience of working in the Hooseland Public Service, we often have a lot more words than actions.

Righto, so actions – let's keep it simple to start and stick to three really strong ones to start this year (trust me you never want to give policy anything too complicated, they will build that feature in themselves...), the simpler it is the greater the chance of it actually getting implemented. First off let's start working on a serious effort to switch to renewable sources of energy, you know, stop using fossil fuels, develop carbon sinks (all those trees the public want to see planted) and create sustainable energy resources (no, that isn't three, I am counting these as one action).

Second, many of our most important crops are at risk, so developing a resilient food future that will support farmers to practice sustainable, climate-smart food production as well as ending current practice will be critically harmed by climate change.

Third, we need to invest in ramping up the efficiency of water use, we have more falling out of the sky than we can handle while at the same time global drinking water supplies are dwindling. We need to be building resilient infrastructure such as ways of capturing rainwater runoff, water treatment plants, and integrating climate-related risks such as floods and droughts into our planning decisions.

That lot would be a starter for ten in proving to Hooselanders that the Government they voted in is *actually* listening! And if it puts us ahead of other western nations, then wouldn't it be a fine thing to be known for globally, rather than our infamy as the fastest to agree to international agreements, but the last to actually ratify them?

As a large and wealthy nation Hooseland has the resources, the will of the people, and finally, a progressive (?) Government needed to lead on climate change and work with other like-minded nations to collectively determine the future of this amazing planet. Failing, that perhaps reconsider my tongue in cheek plan to give everyone a dose of LSD, as your election slogan went, "Let's aim as high as we can Hooseland"!

Yours in service to the public,

Amber Guette

Amber Guette (she/her)

I am Relevant in the Workplace

Dear Minister

For this month's letter I thought I would try to give you some background on the issues we face in the Hooseland Public Service as a workforce. For the most part they are a pretty capable bunch (of course there are always exceptions to every rule), however much Steve in IT likes to joke that the perfect t-shirt for the public service would read "We employ them so you don't have to", (but I know he really doesn't mean it, because he always turns up to Friday night drinks, and they are not compulsory by any means).

Like many workforces we reflect society so of course we have individuals with varying degrees of capability. If anything exacerbates this in the public service, it would have to be the Higher-ups. I know that probably seems lazy, very simple to blame management, but when it comes down to it you cannot blame the incompetent for hiring themselves! I thought I would highlight for you some of the more interesting behaviours I have observed over the years and the creative solutions public servants have come up with to get around them.

One of my favourites was the day I came across a colleague who apparently constituted a whole team on his own, as the 'Contingent Workforce Engineers Department'. I was desperately trying to get approval for a temp as our administrator went on sick leave and just never came back, and we were drowning in overdue reports and compliance box ticking forms. I could not understand why HR were not progressing our request, so I called to investigate, only to be told I had not cleared my request with the 'Contingent Workforce Engineers Department'. I explained I had not cleared it with them as I did not know they even existed!

I got off the phone and asked my colleagues if they knew about them, and oddly *no one* had ever heard of them. I eventually found 'them' working in the basement of the building. It was one rather elderly gentleman who seemed pretty startled that I had found him and wanted to know who had sent me. He was also by default the Manager of the Contingent Workforce Engineers Department. I got my approval to recruit on the understanding that I would not go advertising where he sat. Seems he had been enjoying his anonymity – as very few knew he existed he rarely got asked to do anything.

This brings me to some of the Higher-ups in the Hooseland Public Service that have quite literally taken my breath away at times, as they seem to be of so very little added value. I touched on these in my earlier letter on the Matryoshka doll theory of public management (surely you recall that nice centipede song of Steve's I shared?). We sometimes refer to these sorts of Higher-ups as the 'Windsock Managers', as they tend to be always going in the direction of the biggest blowhard above them and change direction according to their whims.

As a university student at the Hooseland National University doing political science and international relations, I learnt few concepts that I could apply in the real world, but there was one concept that really helped me understand the mindset of some Higher-ups. This was the theory that the two basic principles of American foreign policy were to be explained as follows:

1. America is safer if the rest of the world looks and sounds the same as them; and
2. Americans believe that inside every foreigner is an American just waiting to come out.

This can be nicely applied to the average Higher-up (I say average because some of them are actually pretty good and above average, so this does not apply to them). So, the two basic principles of Higher-ups would look like this:

1. A Higher-up is safe if the rest of the workforce looks and sounds the same as them; and
2. Higher-up's believe that inside every employee is a Higher-up just waiting to come out.

The main problem seems to be that some of them think we really *do* want their job, which could not be further from the truth. I will illustrate this with a few examples of the behaviour of these Higher-ups.

In one job we had the misfortune of having to provide a *lot* of paperwork in hard copy, as it was going to a Minister who did not like digital versions (ironically it was a Minister for the Environment). Keeping these documents in a semblance of order required the use of rather large industrial sized stapler. Which was fine when our team worked next to the legal team as we could always borrow theirs. Fast forward six months and we get moved across the road in one of the many re-stacks needed to accommodate more people with less space.

We approached our Higher-up to ask to buy a big stapler of our own. This was met with the advice that we would just need to go across the road and continue to use the legal team's stapler. Why? Because it was $3 over the threshold for items in our department and apparently, they did not want to request permission from *their* Higher-up. Three weeks of running documents across the road in the middle of winter, including during gale-force winds resulting in one of my poor unfortunate colleagues chasing pieces of paper that escaped their grip (we never did find page 156). We had finally had enough. Solution? We set up a fundraiser on the department's intranet to raise money for a big stapler. The forthcoming laughter from the rest of the teams in our department, and the raised eyebrows of their Higher-up convinced our Higher-up that perhaps it might be easier to just get approval after all.

After they left (promoted out of the department after an unfortunate incident at an office party) we inherited a Higher-up we nicknamed 'The Grey Ghost' a pale, humourless individual with a grey wardrobe to match their skin colour and the constant mournful expression on their face. Working for them you learnt very quickly to get *everything* in writing, as they had zero concern about boldly lying if anything went wrong in the team and throwing their subordinates under the bus. They were the most expert of gas lighters who apparently saw anyone doing a good job as being a threat to their own job security, and so did all they could to undermine and sabotage that person's career. I still shudder when I recall my time under their cold gaze.

Another particularly memorable one liked to bully any quiet or shy team members, no doubt because they thought those people would never fight back. Well one day one of them did!

This individual had refused to hand over the phone number of the boyfriend of one of our team who was on leave to this Higher-up as it was given to them for emergencies only, and the requested information most certainly did not count as an emergency. After walking away in a huff this Higher-up then marched back and yelled at the person in front of the team that their "desk was untidy and a disgrace" and that they had to have it sorted before they left work that day. Instead of wilting with shame they followed the Higher-up back to their desk and when asked what they were doing they stated, "just seeing how you manage to keep your desk so tidy – oh those dividers are great, can you order me some please?". This small act of defiance boosted the morale of the team for a week.

The economic cost of demoralised or disengaged public servants, unwilling or unable to do their best work due to the behaviour of their Higher-up is a direct hit to the public who are not receiving a quality service for their tax dollar. This same Higher-up clung to the idea of hierarchy and even went as far as to reprimand staff members for "fraternising" (not the kind that the earlier Higher-up did at the office party, just normal socialising in coffee breaks) with colleagues lower down the pecking order! Office apartheid is alive and well in the Hooseland Public Service.

It is difficult to thrive if your Higher-up is not supportive. However, it is nearly impossible if your Higher-up is a bully, incompetent or selfish. And if in order to escape that person you need to apply for another position then you are dependent on them for a reference, you are stuffed.

The Hooseland Public Service continues to be character-ised by a hierarchical culture where information and communications are used to achieve control. It appears there may be a misalignment between the aspirations of the modern worker and the dominant culture of our public service. Because if you care and take it to heart, when you see these things happening, you can get very dis-illusioned. All of us have stories of colleagues that have started working as enthusiastic, positive, caring public servants and have walked away completely disillusioned and troubled because of the experience.

Perhaps we need new explicit criteria for how we pick people for management roles that goes beyond the ability to use fear as a tool? Or even better, give teams the chance to vote for their Higher-up? That might cause a sea-change in behaviour.

Yours in service to the public,

Amber Guette (she/her)

I'm Gonna Sit Right Down and Write Myself A Letter

Dear Minister

I see you have someone else going full blown stalker and sending you regular mail :) good to know I am not the only one.... Ironically, I seem to be getting the job of drafting your ministerial correspondence responses, according to your office, I am quite good at "getting the tone of them right"! Of course, quite a lot of the responses are going to your new stalker, a *particularly* grumpy member of the public, referred to in the office as 'Mr Nimby', because while he states that he is very supportive of the idea of the new community health centres, he most certainly does not want one in *his* street.

Fitting then, that this month's letter to you will focus on the Ministerial response letters we write on the behalf of Ministers to the public, and why it may take more time than you would likely assume. I still find it mildly amusing how many members of the public think it is actually the *Minister* writing back to them, of course Mr Nimby is under no such illusion, and it seems you are not his only target, his last missive stated: "I've approached three Ministers from your party in the time you have been the Government, and I have to say your latest response is at least an improvement on the previous two from the other Ministers. Those letters consisted of 'cut and paste' chunks of their department's policy. My questions concerned HOW policy was enacted, but that was NOT addressed in the response at all! I question whether any thought had gone into any of those letters. I was quite pleasantly surprised to get a response that *actually* answered my questions in the latest response from a public servant, a rare treat...", high praise indeed....

I imagine most of the public do not understand that Ministers work far harder than they would assume, it is not all kissing babies and cutting ribbons. Minister's electorate offices are also often pretty poorly resourced, compared say to a private sector manager of equal status. However, the ability of the public to be able to put their views to the Government and get a response is basic democracy, so as good keen public servants the Ministerial Team in CHAOS are always happy to help with keeping the lines of communication open with the public.

The job of your office in handling all this incoming correspondence is two-fold. Firstly, because you get *loads* of correspondence, you need to have good staff that can quickly sort out what they think you as the Minister will want to deal with (perhaps because it fits with a bigger point you want to make, or because they know you will genuinely want to help, and can possibly even do some good), and what should get sent to CHAOS (because it needs a more formal reply or requires a technical response from the department).

Of course, both your office and ours have to be careful that we are singing from the same song sheet and not contradicting each other. *All* correspondence is potentially in the public domain and could just as easily be from a newspaper or a political rival on a 'fishing expedition', as it could be a genuine member of the public wanting answers to their burning questions, so this also needs to be front of mind.

Whoever it is that writes on your behalf requires a unique skill set (including the ability to fix a paper jam that requires removing smouldering paper from an overheated photocopier before a fire starts...). For example, are they able to wade through several pages of nearly indecipherable spidery handwriting to get to the heart of the matter in order to discern what it is the writer *really* wants to know?

This is not as straightforward as it seems, and I have seen many newbies get this quite spectacularly wrong. In one instance, a member of the public on a health benefit sent a long letter bemoaning the lack of a level playing field for young people from poorer families getting scholarships, citing the example of her very affluent sister's child getting a scholarship without the financial need, but with the same grades as *her* child who missed out.

The resulting draft response had the Minister congratulating them on their niece getting a scholarship! Completely missed the point and would have quite likely really enraged the recipient and confirmed their likely suspicions that all Ministers have a Marie Antoinette 'let them eat cake' complex (this complex can be glaringly obvious when Ministers get asked what they think the median salary is or the ubiquitous favourite of journos worldwide, what does a loaf of bread cost).

The best writers know how to put themselves in the shoes of the requester and show a bit of empathy, speaking of which, my other pet hate in draft replies is the old 'pass the buck' mentality some political advisors and public servants have. With very little extra effort on their behalf that person could find out quite easily from their colleagues in another department *exactly* what the requester needs to know, time for a bit of the old 'buck stops here' attitude to the public's questions instead.

When communicating in any way with the public it is essential that bureaucratic jargon is avoided at all costs.

The public *hates* bureaucratic jargon, it is overbearing, patronising and pointless. As is the use of the passive voice. Passive voice in these situations just shows a lack of accountability. Let's be honest here, Ministers often use it to act as if these mistakes were things that happened outside of their control. But that's often not true, is it?

If the aim of the game is to increase accountability, legitimacy and trust in governments, then it would be much better for a reply to admit to a mistake being made, how it happened and how it will be prevented from happening in the future. I can only imagine how irritating it must be for the public to get a cheerful offer of help after we have just singularly failed to provide it, we need to own the fact that they have been let down before we offer the solution.

Now as a rule, most public servants do not deliberately seek to complicate the information they present for your responses. Writing Ministerial responses is more of a team effort with the incoming from your office going through a coordinator who decides which writer will 'hold the pen' (be responsible for the overall response in gov speak).

These writers then draft the replies, based on the facts provided by the Subject Matter Experts (SMEs) elsewhere in the department who are familiar with the issues raised in the incoming letter.

It is also crucial of course that we are aware of any previous correspondence, written parliamentary questions or requests under the Act on the topic of the letter, as well as how any new developments, or the passing of time may have changed the messaging on that particular topic. It is not uncommon for a draft reply that was completely accurate when it was written, to be wrong by the time it reaches a Minister for signing in 20 days' time.

Although errors of spelling or punctuation are *usually*

spotted and corrected during the lengthy approval process through which all ministerial correspondence passes, occasionally something gets missed and once it is too late someone realises, that for want of a hyphen, the Minister has signed and sent a letter noting that "The Chair of the Board has decided to resign their employment contract" instead of "The Chair of the Board has decided to re-sign their employment contract."

More significantly, an incorrect date or inaccurate financial total (frightening how a decimal point in the wrong spot can go completely missed after a six-person peer review process...) in a letter could have serious legal and political repercussions for a Minister.

On top of all this, government departments often service several Ministers, each Minister requiring an individual feel for their correspondence, reflecting the personal image or 'tone' that they wish to project. This tone can significantly modify the overall style of a letter.

Some Ministers prefer a business-like tone, requesting that we avoid being too familiar, or friendly in their correspondence (or in one rather puzzling instance the words "thank you").

Another Minister may consider that we owe the taxpaying citizen a warm, fair and reasonable response to their query. A draft reply for such a Minister would be warmer in tone, beginning "Dear [First name], Thank you for your letter of ..."; and to continue with empathetic lines such as "I am pleased to inform you that..." or "Unfortunately... "; and end with something along the lines of "I hope this information is useful to you" or "I appreciate your writing to me about this matter." So, as you can see from the above the whole process is a *wee* bit more complicated than either a Minister or the public might imagine....

On the positive side of things correspondence can be a very effective way for a Minister to make contact with a wide range of the public, often private citizens write letters to Ministers because they have no other easy means of direct access to those who are governing our country (pretty much why I am writing to you directly). A thorough and well-written personal response to such letters will reassure the recipient that their concerns are being dealt with by a responsive and responsible Minister who deserves to remain in power, and surely that is the aim of the game.

Yours in service to the public,

Amber Guette (she/her)

Lookin' Out for No.1

Dear Minister

Mid-summer in Hooseland, which means more than half the government are away on holiday! Things are definitely heating up in Hooseland this summer – another year of record highs. Speaking of heating up, I want to discuss the explosion in the number of political advisers in Minister's offices these days.

While the current Government has been very public about wanting to be more transparent (not really a *very* high bar after the previous Government's games of cloak and dagger), evidence suggests the political advisers (often wannabe politicians in training) in your office never got that particular memo.... Why all the drama you may be thinking? Read on....

At times I feel really sorry for the CHAOS Department's Private Secretaries working in your office. As the representatives of our department working in your office at parliament they are often caught between a rock and a hard place. We are working hard at CHAOS to meet the Government's expectations of transparency and carry out our work on that basis.

But when it gets sent to our Private Secretary in your office their heart sinks. They read what we have provided and know full well how your political advisers will react, so every worst-case scenario is flashing through their mind. They have told me they actually go into a cold sweat when they place the documents in the political adviser's in-tray....

Here is a verbatim example of their behaviour: My phone rings, it is Raphael, our current Private Secretary in your office, "What is this that you have sent over in the Minister's daily bag!? Why are you providing x & y in this response to a request from the Opposition – it will open a whole can of worms – I can't take this to the political advisers – they will hit the roof!"

"Good morning to you too. Hey, I know it is new territory, but the Minister has been pretty clear on expectations around this stuff", "Oh yes, I am well aware of that, but the political advisers think transparency is over rated and will just see nothing but risk in this – they will jump all over me and want answers to all their questions from me immediately – you don't know how bad it is over here!".

I told him to tell them to ring *me* with any questions, but it goes deeper than that, and I wish you would talk to them. They need to understand that your publicly proclaimed position on transparency is being watched very closely, (particularly by the Opposition) and if they really want to be paranoid, they can try being paranoid about making you look like promises made in opposition amount to nothing now that you are in power.

Look, we get it, political advisers in Ministers` offices are here to stay and truth be told I have worked with some delightful political advisers in the past – they were engaged and communicated well with the department, they ensured clarity and even added to the transparency between the Minister and the department.

We understand the pressures they face working in a Ministerial office, and that it is our job to ensure the political advisers get early advice on issues which could be problematic for you. Unfortunately, the current bunch in your office do not seem to understand that having a good relationship with the department is part of their job.

They have developed a reputation for bullying the poor private secs by treating them as the punching bag for all the things they don't like about CHAOS.

Behaviour such as not letting them in to meetings on important issues – but then blaming them for not knowing when a decision has been made, making them sit isolated in a corner of the office while they all sit in a cosy group on the other side of the office – knowledge is power in a Minister's office, they know this and are using it to their advantage.

The levels of artificial stress created by the political adviser's behaviour is making the role of private secretary in your office a poisoned chalice, which will only lower the quality of candidates willing to go over there. It used to be an exciting career opportunity – now we struggle to find anyone willing to do it.

As a senior official I have had them blatantly lie about work I had done – claiming I had not sent it to them, and that lie made it to the highest levels of our department. Thank goodness I know the only safeguard in the public service is to keep ALL your emails… that cleared me of all allegations – but of course no apology was given….

Amongst the many things I have seen them doing, perhaps the most dangerous was ignoring our departmental responses to your parliamentary questions from the Opposition last month and providing the *exact* opposite information to you because it "sounded better"!?!

Not very clever when the Opposition is then likely going to request something that just does not exist…. That's the trouble with 'spin', it doesn't take much to knock it off its axis, and then it gets out of control pretty quick. Anyhow, adding fuel to the fire, they did not bother to tell *us* they had changed the response, so the next time we got that question we are (inadvertently) putting you at risk with our (truthful) response.

My prediction is that this will come back to bite us all. And from now on until it goes away it will be a never-ending source of annoyance for those of us that have to keep responding to the probing of the Opposition on this subject....

I guess their bullying and Machiavellian ways may even pay off for you at times, but it also lacks integrity and brings great risk with it.

They are not public servants like you and I, they are in no-man's land, and they are a law unto themselves. Their career progress is paramount, and they will throw anyone under the bus that gets in their way. I guess that is politics.

So, I am asking you, *please* look after our people, and try a little harder to set expectations with your staff if you really mean what you say about transparency. As a Minister you have a big part to play in setting the tone of relations between political advisers and public servants here in Hooseland. How can you do that?

For a starter, you need to make it clear to them that political advisers *cannot* give directions to departmental public servants. Our TOTP has made it very clear to us that any advice that does not come through the correct channels is not to be followed. While political advisers are at liberty to make comments to their Minister about departmental advice, they are not there to be 'gate-keepers' deciding what you see.

I see there is a proposal being tabled for a legislated code of conduct for workers in Parliament. This is long overdue but bear in mind that just like in the public service codes of conduct are not enough to change the behaviour of political advisers. It is tone at the top that changes behaviours.

I was discussing the problem of rogue political advisers with a Higher-up once and they advised me that they had dealt with a political adviser who had told them that the Minister was not interested in receiving any further advice on a particular issue.

The Higher-up asked if that was the Ministers actual opinion or theirs? They replied that it was the same thing.... Turned out it was not the same thing, and fortunately for that Higher-up they knew the issue was key to achieving a vital part of government policy, and they kept a watching brief on the issue and raised it again in a face-to-face with the Minister, it was new news to the Minister, and they were very grateful to receive it as it solved a major headache for them at the time.

Political advisers need to appreciate that Ministerial decision-making can only benefit by being exposed to the evidence-based research that seasoned public servants can bring to an issue. In the end, whatever is specified in codes of conduct, legislated or otherwise, the relationships between Ministerial offices and departments will only work if Ministers make clear the behaviour they expect from their staff.

Yours in service to the public,

Amber Guette (she/her)

The Fletcher Memorial Home

Dear Minister

Historically the start of Autumn heralded the annual Hooseland Public Service Integrity and Behaviour Audit, and our small talk in the office would have been less small and more about that, but mysteriously all trace of this seems to have disappeared from the Hooseland Public Service Intranet.

So, in a spirit of service to my colleagues, I decided to take matters into my own hands and do my own survey. Giving public servants a voice on what they think matters, so for this one I decided to focus specifically on what my colleagues think makes for good and bad Higher-ups (especially as some of them aspire to those roles), so I created a SurveyBadger survey to get some anonymous feedback from a range of public servants across Hooseland.

I have picked a random sample of the replies to give you a sense of the mood on the front lines, and I am starting with what makes for bad Higher-ups first, so that we can finish this letter on a positive note with the good ones. Here goes!

Q. What, in your honest opinion, are the worst qualities of public service Higher-ups?

A. "A bad Higher-up is rarely caught out, they just seem to get reshuffled! My top three worst qualities are micro-management, not taking an interest in public servants' professional development, and poor communication.

Micro-managers get in the way of their team members daily job, and I reckon this is a trait of insecure managers who think it counts as a managerial skill."

A. "Higher-ups who selectively enforce the rules, for example our bootlicker deputy team leader can go for thirty-minute smoke breaks, whereas the other team members get sarcastic comments for taking more than a second extra in their 15-minute break. No consistency."

A. "Credit hogging sociopaths that fail to action items for days, then send them out as urgent at 3pm Friday, with the work due first thing Monday morning with zero context and the guarantee of either a. Public humiliation when they email everyone about what a crap job that one person did, or b. Taking all the credit for a job well done, without a nod to the team of dedicated employees duck-paddling like crazy to make it work."

A. "I had one who shot down any improvement ideas I came up with, basically saying "that's just how it is around here". The same person also did the bare minimum response when asked questions, and when I left the department couldn't be bothered to wish me luck, thank me for my time, or even acknowledge that I had earned the promotion."

A. "A Higher-up who is not accountable for failures. Blames the team for objectives that were not met. Makes the employees grind hardcore until there is nothing left... Only burnt-out public servants."

A. "The behaviours I've seen in Higher-ups can be attributed to insecurity. It causes micro-management, incomplete communication, mixed messages, emotional outbursts, clock-watching, or insistence on trivial and pointless processes. These are all behaviours used to mask the fact that they don't feel like they know or understand what is happening or are confident that they can speak to what their team does."

A. "Trying so hard to show their value they don't listen to anyone else, fake sincerity, talking authoritatively about stuff they have no clue about, eye rolling and shrugging and being dismissive."

A. "Two opposing worst types of Higher-ups I've had: The first one took all the credit for the work, despite not actually participating in any way (didn't show up for meetings, didn't provide guidance, didn't even review the work before sending it up). Also played favourites.

The second one in complete contrast did all the work, and constantly complained about it. Never delegated to the team because the team members were "not competent enough" but the same manager "didn't have time to train them."

A. "Yep, worst are micro-managers. Also, those that don't defend you when needed or are very harsh when you've made a one-off mistake. Micromanaging is out of control in the Hooseland Public Service."

A. "Seat warmers who don't want to rock the boat and choose inaction and allow their staff to "figure things out". No direction and or actual management of their teams. What is worse, they become 'blockers' and they actively cause reverse workflows and additional work."

A. "Higher-ups who interfere in work tasks, such as withholding needed information, undermining or sabotage. This I find truly sinister and is something that Higher-ups tend to pull on anyone who is considered a rival, or someone they need to find any excuse to get rid of.

Most of the time the victim is not made aware that it is occurring until they are made to look a fool. The key problem is that many of those who aspire to middle-management cannot fathom that most people would rather gnaw their own arms off than have such roles – in other words the competent people around them are not a threat because they don't want their jobs – they just want the real work to be done well, regardless of any impediments from Higher-ups."

Okay, that about covers it for the negatives... personally, I recognise the behaviours described above, and have worked with some of these types. I have also had the pleasure of meeting some brilliant Higher-ups like Susan H, in my career, and they are exceptionally valuable public assets. They are committed to high levels of care and service, are considerate and supportive of their staff, and are loyal to their department's missions and values. So, let's hear what our public servants think are the qualities of the best Higher-ups.

Q. *What makes for a good Higher-up?*

A. "Humanity. Understanding fairness. Confidence in their own decisions. Lesser Higher-ups just don't have this."

A. "Have lots of knowledge about what their team does, you can even ask them specialist questions and they'll know the answer. Typically, these rare gems are Higher-ups who started as lowly advisers and have worked their way up into low to mid-tier management over the last 5 to 10 years, thus have a ton of field experience and knowledge".

A. "They are likeable, caring, compassionate and approachable. A good Higher-up doesn't have to be exactly all four of these qualities, but the better the Higher-up is the more likely they are to have all of these qualities. A good one knows when to be firm with enforcing the rules, while always being fair".

A. "Tend to be hands off with their management, not wanting

to impede their team members with unnecessary micromanagement, if the Higher-up is really good, they'll be looking for solutions to problems that are expressed in team meetings or in one on ones".

A. "Higher-ups who basically say, you're an adult. You've got stuff to do, I've got stuff to do. Here when you need me. Those are the best managers I've had".

A. "Collaborative, open, and supportive Higher-ups who encourage professional development, recognise good work, play to their employee's talents, and lead with compassion".

A. "My last Higher-up was amazing at being transparent and willing to "go to bat" to retain great people. I left the org for another one, but it wasn't for her lack of trying".

A. "Self-assurance (and I mean the real stuff, not fake pretence thereof) is the one thing that makes a huge difference. Self-assurance also means that they can handle employee departure like adults because they don't have a deep-seated fear that without the employee, they will lose all expertise and be lost. Instead, they show trust, give people more responsibilities, and help them grow. And people who are self-assured don't need constant reassurance via praise and yes-men. Their ego is stable, and they can handle being told I think you're wrong and here is why without throwing a tantrum. In fact, they will appreciate it. One tell-tale sign of a good self-assured Higher-up: they take the blame when things go bad and make employees shine when things go well".

A. "Empowering the team, listening, trusting, providing support in a constructive way, sharing the glory, encouraging growth and moving up even if it means moving elsewhere, actually caring about the people".

A. "Higher-ups with vision who can acknowledge that

they don't know everything and that there is room for growth".

A. "Find a Higher-up that can take risks and assume the consequences if it fails. Everything else becomes secondary".

So now that we have a clearer picture of the qualities we need in our Hooseland Higher-ups, how do we sort the wheat from the chaff? I think a good place to start could be a full 360-degree performance assessment of all Higher-ups by their whole team.

People who perform poorly in how they manage people should be denied promotion in people management roles. When public servants see people who systematically behave badly not being promoted, getting demoted or even losing their job, behaviour *will* change.

Perhaps the most important trait of a good Higher-up is being self-aware and recognising what their own strengths and weaknesses are. Then they can build up a team that can compensate for any weaknesses and complement their strengths.

Finally, all this needs transparency and collaboration. Being clear about what behaviours are promoted in a department will have an impact. What has been missing in the Hooseland Public Service is a commitment to leadership development at all levels, and this no doubt contributes to why leadership in the public service is patchy at best.

Yours in service to the public,

Amber Guette (she/her)

I Am Not a Blocker

Dear Minister

I see you are having problems with the Opposition blocking your new bill in the House? Rather frustrating, isn't it? And you have to question their motives as this *definitely* seems like something they would normally be backing if they were in power.

The struggle of having to deal with blockers is a reality for those of us in the Hooseland Public Service as well, so this month I want to share with you some of the tips and tricks I have found over the years for dealing with this disturbing behaviour.

To be honest I kind of enjoy the challenge of navigating the blockers in the Hooseland Public Service as they happily put up their impediments to progress. Of course, these behaviours are not limited to the public service, and every workplace has one or more of these delights.

As we go about our work serving the public, our job is not to tolerate this often-self-serving behaviour, but to figure out how to deal with them (my instinct is a bulldozer but only on my bad days). They may even think they are coming from a place of good not evil, especially if in their heads they are protecting their busy Higher-up from more work, and sometimes they are actually just fulfilling the wishes of a Higher-up and have been *instructed* to stall, or actually even stop, progress on a piece of work because of information that the Higher-up is privy to but is not willing or able to share.

This is more common than you think, and often sees

public servants continuing on the path of trying to progress the work because they are not aware it will never be given the green light – which leads to a major waste of time, effort and Hooseland taxpayer's dollars, all because it would never enter their minds to just say "you don't need to know why right now, but that piece of work cannot be progressed at present so just park it and focus on other work".

In the interests of trying to be solution focused, I will outline the various types of workplace blockers and share some strategies on how to deal with them. Let's start with the one who actually has the decision-making power. In my experience, these individuals are often a challenge worth tackling, mostly because they don't usually start from a place of insecurity or anxiety over progress, after all they did not get to the position of decision maker by sitting on their hands (or at least most didn't...).

These blockers require a delicate touch, and with a bit of positive messaging you can often make them think it was their idea all along (let's be honest, if it turns out to be a *really* good idea, they will take ownership of it anyway).

A second blocker you will more likely encounter is the person that does not have the power to decide but does have the power to play gatekeeper. These are a bit of a nightmare to be honest. Often, they are in a position just ahead of you in the pecking order and are likely to wield that power like their life depends on it. For these blockers the old saying 'if at first you don't succeed try, try and try again' comes into play.

Firstly, make your approach by email never by phone. You are going to need those written records to prove you have followed correct procedure in trying to get their assistance and tugged your forelock the requisite number of times.

If this does not work, try going around them – is there any other avenue you can use to make progress? No? Now is the time to take a deep breath and go over them – if the issue is an IT or HR one, then go straight to the head of that division.

It will not win you friends with the blocker, but sometimes it is the only way to get them to engage with the issue. This could of course land you in hot water, but as long as you can prove your intent was good and you were just trying to do the job you are paid to do as efficiently as possible, the blow-back should not be too bad.

Not feeling like you want to risk your career like that? There is one more solution. If none of the above work or appeal to you, is there likely someone in the department that is seen as an 'influencer' or power broker? This might be a highly respected Higher-up in another team, proud of their accomplishments, protective of their turf, vain enough to enjoy the fact that you need their help, but smart enough to see that if your idea is a good one, it will benefit them to be seen to be promoting it.

Finally, remember those canny Canadians I introduced you to in the first few months of my letters? Well, they have something more to say about dealing with blockers, or as the Canadians call them, 'Roadblocks'. I will leave you with some of their wisdom via more direct quotes from that public servant's bible – Scheming Virtuously for Public Servants:

- When you hit a roadblock, keep track of the 'why's' and 'by who's'. This will allow you to streamline your delivery and better anticipate potential blockages in the future. It also shows that you are learning from the process and gives your work more credibility.
- The first time you make a mistake, plug the holes. The next time you make that same mistake you deserve to sink because what you should have done was build a better boat.
- When building support, strategy and sequence become

incredibly important. When you are shopping for support go after the key influencers in your department and make them champions, unofficial or otherwise. You know who these people are – when they speak others listen.

- You should approach the early adopters first. Isolate the roadblocks and – keep them out of the equation for as long as possible.

- Find the people in your organisation that see the value of what you are doing. Moreover, try to get a few of the key influencers who can help bring people down off the fence or exert pressure on those typically

- Once you have a critical mass, approach the naysayers. Show them what you are proposing, show them your support base, and ask for their participation. The more pressure you can bring to bear on the naysayers, the less likely they are to continue saying nay."

Working with a blocker and gaining support is never a quick fix, it requires patience and time, and you will need to move your chess pieces strategically. You will need to try and understand what it is your blocker wants to achieve by their behaviour and then using that knowledge, try to change the focus from 'I want' to 'you need', well at least in their minds that is.

To give you an example of how doing this works in the real world, I offer you the following example. I recall watching the worst blocking behaviour in one particularly siloed Hooseland Public Service agency. One of the smaller groups in the department needed a policy product from the much larger, and more established policy group as they were forbidden to do their own policy work (due to the existence of the larger group, who were supposedly responsible for providing policy products for the whole of the department).

The smaller, requesting group only needed one product. The brick wall in this instance was the long-standing Higher-up of the larger group who protected their turf with ferocity and declared they did not have time for the smaller groups request, and that it did not fit within their perceived priorities. The individual in need of this group's offerings took the time to tune in to the background and find out a way to get what they needed.

They discovered the loose brick in this wall was their need to be seen as being at the cutting edge of things in the sector. The head of the smaller department got the Chair of a particularly powerful Board in the sector to raise the need for the policy product with the TOTP in the department, which meant that the request then came from there as well as from the smaller group. I can happily report that things moved pretty quickly and painlessly once that loose brick was discovered, and the required policy product was delivered well within the necessary timeframe for the smaller group to deliver their work.

Of course, when it comes to blockers you will need to pick and choose the tactics and approaches for your situation, however, a bit of creative thinking when it comes to blockers can go a long way.

In the example above, there would have been no action if the Higher-up of the larger group did not perceive it as being of material interest to their own goals. These people have a lot of power and are the hardest blockers to deal with but learning how to handle them ensures you are going to find handling the blockers lower down the hierarchy a lot easier....

Yours in service to the public,

Amber Guette (she/her)

The Way It Is

Dear Minister

Not a great week. This may be my last letter to you as I am starting to think my taking this risk and being honest with you is landing on deaf ears.

It has been over two years since I started telling you about the state the Hooseland Public Service is in, and not only is nothing getting any better, but I actually think it may be getting worse! I look around at my fellow public servants and it just feels like we continue to lurch from one bad situation to another. And if we raise any of this with Higher-ups, we are told it is just the way it is and to get used to it.

So, a quick refresher on the main issues we continue to face today, under your Government. If you can only solve one problem at a time, then please make bullying the first – if any one thing *has to happen* it is putting an end to a culture of bullying in the Hooseland Public Service.

We are all very weary of working in an environment whereby managing up and pleasing the Minister is valued but managing people and culture and dealing with poor performance is not. This misaligned management culture pretty much feeds in to all the daily nightmares public servants face in the workplace. Of course, it is not just the behaviour but the work environment in which it is happening.

Last year's Hooseland Public Service survey found that nearly 55% of public servants were having to do the same or more work, but with fewer resources. At the same time 25% felt they were being expected to work to unreasonable deadlines. Work overload is now the reality for many public servants. This leads to us juggling highly complex workloads, with little time to reflect and plan our work, keeping us on a treadmill that never feels like we are making the difference we joined to make in the first place.

Adding to that sense of not being able to make a difference, is the volume of unnecessary work (the bit that the public call out as bureaucracy) required by Higher-ups but adding nothing to the public good. Look, we get it, all the extra process is there to 'cover our butts', and we want to be accountable. But sometimes the box ticking cannot be justified, making it even more demoralising, (and yes I am looking at you Programme Office...)

Added to the box ticking are the so called 'targets' that we are expected to meet. Again, these would be fine if they related in any way to the real-world priorities for our work. So much for these targets claiming to be "S.M.A.R.T targets (Specific, Measurable, Achievable, Realistic and Timely...).

Higher-ups need to understand that we need to be trusted, not micromanaged. Having a lack of control over how we meet our goals at work can really ruin any chance for job satisfaction – if we can see what needs to be done, but do not have the autonomy to do it, we just end up feeling like some kind of a robot with zero input into making a difference and no opportunity to show real initiative in our work. This is all fed into by Higher-ups paralysing risk aversion on the behalf of the department. Risk taking can be a vital aspect of feeling trusted to be able to do the right thing for public servants.

Constantly changing government priorities (yes, yes, I know 'ambiguity') coupled with a lack of opportunity is another major source of frustration. Much of the time we are having to be reactive in our work – the proverbial 'ambulance at the bottom of the cliff' which means opportunities for being strategic and working 'upstream' to prevent the issues in the first instance are very hard to come by, negating the reason most of us signed up to be public servants in the first place.

And once you finally get a piece of work done the real work is often just beginning for those of us at the coalface, the dreaded approval process in very hierarchical departments is often the reason that items are late.

Compounding this, rigid hierarchies can lead to too much distance between leadership and those doing the doing of the work. The TOTP can appear distant, and unapproachable – trust is a big issue in hierarchies. To their credit some TOTP's work to break the mould and encourage public servants to call them by their first name rather than by their titles, taking time to walk the floor so that they can make informal contact, and get to know people on an individual level, and all of those little personal touches make a huge amount of difference to morale.

It is often the case that the time pressure makes everything, even something as simple as sending an email, riskier. We had one such incident in CHAOS, which even though it was *very* amusing for the office at the time, one external email address in the very long chain of 'reply all's could have made it a disaster for a colleague of the sender. No one had any idea it was anything other than just another boring office email and would no doubt not have even noticed if it had not been for the urgently sent MESSAGE RECALL that we received. Of course, then it became the most interesting thing in our inbox to read.

Scrolling down it became clear why it had been recalled.... Buried at the bottom of the email was an email from one colleague to another venting along the lines of "Thank *you* very much, it's been a full-on week this week with some incredibly vexatious or long-winded, deep-diving queries. Still breathing fire over that Hooseland Clarion story. Total crock of s**t!!! And they know it!!!!! Sigh". It was a simple matter of the colleague who received this then sending a further email without deleting the email chain below it. Could happen to anyone and most of us have felt our blood turn to ice-water at least once in our career after hitting send... public servants are humans too, but lord help them if they had let that email escape the building....

I know I have spoken about silos before, but since we are recapping it is important to note that they have an effect on the people as well as the process. We are either drowning in too much process, or *desperately* trying to find some method to the madness (most of us just give up once we realise that if a process did exist, it has been ignored or replaced with work arounds to speed things up.

Even within CHAOS, our finance systems do not interface with our HR Systems, and neither interface with payroll.... We have ministerial servicing tools that are used by one team, but not another in the same unit, it all starts to make Mandarin style bureaucracy look almost attractive – at least they probably know what the heck is going on.

While some of the Higher-ups think that a cut-throat environment and a culture of fear ensures engagement (and sometimes even excitement), research proves that the inevitable stress it creates will likely lead to burnout and disengagement over the long-term. Research proves that workplace stress in the Hooseland Public Service has led to an increase of almost 58% in voluntary turnover.

A Hooseland Clarion poll showed that, when offered benefits such as flexitime and work-from-home opportunities, public servants preferred workplace well-being over material benefits. When our Higher-ups realise that by prioritising positive, supportive, work cultures they can have the reflected glory of much higher levels of financial performance, measurable progress in departmental outcomes, greater productivity, and employee engagement, then maybe then they will realise that if they really want to 'please the Minister', that is the best way to do it!

If any of this is not getting through, or if you do not see any value in my continuing to write to you each month then remember you can always leave the red flag up on your letterbox Tuesday next month and I will take it as confirmation that I should discontinue my missives. Until then, as always,

Yours in service to the public,

Amber Guette (she/her)

An Insult to The Fact Checkers

Dear Minister

Winter is just around the corner, but I am made all the warmer by not seeing the red flag up when I went to deliver this month's letter. I saw that your firewood had been delivered, so it looks like you are well prepared for the coming cold at least.

Unfortunately, prepared is one thing you can never be when you start your first job in the Hooseland Public Service. So that is going to be the theme of this month's letter – what it is like to work in the public service.

I enjoyed sharing the free and frank feedback from the survey of my fellow public servants at the start of summer in the Fletcher Memorial letter, and as you hear *more* than enough from me on my experiences, I am going to share with you an interview I did with a first-rate public servant on their experiences in the Hooseland Public Service.

They are a consummate professional and have made major contributions over the course of their career, they survived a very tough childhood, got their degree as a psychologist, bought their own home, and even more impressive, they did all this as a single parent. Look up 'Resilient' in the dictionary and you will see their picture. Please bear all that in mind as you read about their experiences in the Hooseland Public Service.

A> Thanks for agreeing to do this M, it was not easy to find someone willing to speak, even anonymously. Let's start with the best job you have had in the Hooseland Public Service?

M> Probably psych service for the Hooseland Correctional Services, working as a cognitive behavioural therapist.

A> What was your worst job?

M> Department of Social Services. Working as the lead sexual violence adviser.

A> And why was it the worst job, what were the elements that made it the worst? Was it the work itself, or the environment?

M> Oh I loved the work. It was the environment – toxic management was not only excused but encouraged. Some of these people, who were meant to be there to help people, well their egos were completely out of control, and because of their behaviour really good people, people who were making a difference in the very difficult work on sexual violence, were put in a position where they had to leave.

A> Do you feel your career in the Hooseland Public Service has created value in your life?

M> At times, I believe bringing a psychological treatment element into roles like the National Crime Agency, and the Department of Justice has added value. Because a lot of those roles before that were purely based around academic points of law, so bringing in treatment options and therapeutic courts was a big deal.

We were told at the time that it was crazy, but now it has become the norm, and it was just a small group of like-minded people that made it happen. It was good back then, the Hooseland Public Service was actually acknowledged as a good profession. I had great Higher-ups at the National Crime Agency, that was all before it got so risk averse.

Our policy was absolutely taken on board by the Government. The Minister loved it and asked us to look at designing all of the Hooseland justice system along those lines.

But nowadays, it's so political. Having and expressing new and innovative ideas is not encouraged, you're not allowed to fail. They pretend you are, but now if you fail it's embarrassing. You've bought scorn on the Government.

Whereas when I first started, some of those ideas from a psychological point of view, were allowed to be trialled and if they failed, they just failed. No issue, whereas now it's just like 'no we cannot do that, what would the Minister say?"

A> So it's the politicisation of the Hooseland Public Service?

M> Yeah, that's what has taken away the ability of public servants to make a real difference and be honest about things.

In the past I had been able to say what the unintended consequences were going to be when a Minister had a dumb idea. So, for me the most frustrating job I had was the drug reform legislation. That was done at speed without looking at the unintended consequences, even though we raised red flags and asked for a proper timeline that allowed for research and consultation with the community and experts in this area. And now when you look at where we are, it was obviously wrong for this to be pushed ahead quickly to meet a political need, it clearly does not serve the long-term best interest of the Hooseland public.

A> Why do you think we did not focus taxpayers' money on ensuring that the right legislation was passed?

M> No idea, it seemed crazy to be picking on otherwise law-abiding people for using marijuana, instead of focusing on much more dangerous anti-social illegal drugs. And for me, it was knowing the amount of harmful drugs out there, if you look at all of the intel on what is coming in to Hooseland from imports. We are not even touching the sides of the problem.

This is where the ideology and the rhetoric were getting in the way of actual good policy advice. But lord help you if you spoke up and criticised the Government. And you quickly learn that if you don't have the same thinking as the Government of the day, you are frozen out amongst your colleagues.

This was the first time in my career that I could just not *believe* that we had people in the room that knew better, but actually allowed a daft idea to go ahead. Just sitting there, letting it grow legs, because nobody wanted to speak up and say this is ridiculous, to say it will not work. If you say there are any issues with the policy, then you're seen as just being negative. As a senior policy adviser, I cannot believe we've got into this situation, where we pretend we're more open and honest and engaging, and I just don't see that at all.

A> It's sounds like the consultation on that policy just became a box ticking exercise?

M> It's feels like it was never to actually learn a lesson, or to see what other perspectives there are on something, and the cynicism was just so depressing. I also find it ironic that we're willing to risk our integrity as public servants for political reasons.

That's one of the most infuriating things for me, there's a couple of things happening here. One of them is you feel like you are not doing your job as a public servant because you are not able to provide free and frank advice without fear or favour.

And this is the most important part, if I really am calling out a Minister, it is in *their best interest*. If you let them go and do stuff that you know could be politically damaging or that is not in the best interests of the public, how can that be okay? I don't understand why we can't just be straight up with them.

A> Did you ever consider whistleblowing?

M> Yes, I considered it a couple of times. Once when the National Crime Agency started to move away from a victim focus to focusing on nothing but the offender. But I probably got the closest when I worked for the Department of Social Services, not just for my sanity, but for the sake of less strong colleagues, I needed to do a personal grievance against a gas-lighting, sociopathic, narcissistic Higher-up. But we all know the price you pay for being a whistleblower in the Hooseland Public Service. We all know how things work in Hooseland.

A> Thank you again for your honesty M – you may finally have gotten the opportunity to talk truth to power again, at least to one Minister.

Mic drop....

Yours in service to the public,

Amber Guette

Amber Guette (she/her)

RESPECT

Dear Minister

What in the heck is going on with this Government? I could not believe the headlines in the paper this morning!? I know the lines between Ministers and public servants can get blurred at times, but this is full on interference in the public service! And to do this to the Hooseland Integrity Commission – oh the irony…. It feels like everything I have been raising with you over the last couple of years has just gone under the wheels of the Government bus.

Public service neutrality, our supposedly apolitical, non-partisan public service, is not just a 'nice to have' that you can pick and choose to ignore when it suits you. It is *essential* to ensuring that public servants will treat any incoming government in an equitable manner. These values are the underlying scaffolding that hold up justice and continuity in our public service, and directly affect the levels of trust the public have in the Hooseland system of government.

And yet what headline does the nation awaken to? "Hooseland Integrity Commissioner resigns following concerns about interference with his office from the Government." The very person tasked with maintaining the Hooseland Government's register of lobbyists and confidentially advising politicians on integrity matters, and *your* people decide it is a good idea to go after them? That sounds like the very definition of self-sabotage??

The article goes on to say that you ordered the State Services Department to confiscate the Integrity Commission staff's mobile phones and laptops, delete records from those devices, and alter security permissions and access to the Commission's offices, as *retribution* for the Commissioner voicing concern publicly on major cutbacks made to the Commission. The number of staff working at the Commission had already been cut from nine to four, right at a time when major lobbying around the large government projects (I read the CHAOS new state-of-the-art community health centres when I saw that) had attracted the interests of major lobbying bodies from 'Big Pharma' and other vested interest consortia. Coincidence? I think not... and even if it was, how do you think the public will see it?

The Opposition are having a field day with this, pointing out that if the Integrity Commissioner cannot hold the Government to account on really serious integrity issues, then who can? Who indeed...?

Even as I am writing this letter another brave public servant has blown the whistle (and likely ended their career) on the Government's treatment of the Integrity Commission – the midday news on the radio is reporting that a former employee has exposed a culture of secrecy in the public service, stating the Hooseland Public Service is "driven by a culture that prioritises protecting the Government from scrutiny", this is shameful, as much for us public servants as it should be for you Ministers, we have collectively let the Hooseland public down.

This happened on the public services watch – that means *no one* had been standing for what is right in the State Services Department or they would never have let things get this bad....

For more than three hundred years Hooseland has had a reputation for having a professional, politically neutral public service. It was hard won, and it seems our colleagues think they have the right to destroy that? It used to be taken as fact that our TOTP's would act independently of Ministers in all employment matters, including appointments, promotions, or termination of employment. Effective government necessitates both Ministers and public servants being willing to be challenged, able to listen and to work constructively in the best interests of the public – why is that so hard?

Following on from the front-page headlines, page four outlines an email that has been leaked, proving our Secretary of Justice had been enquiring about a senior public servant's political leanings before they were given a role in their office. Another nail in our coffin....

Under the previous Hooseland Government, as the Opposition, you and your colleagues made great mileage out of the scandal regarding a Minister and a TOTP illegally interfering in a public service employment matter, the Minister demanded the termination of a senior public servant, the TOTP not only made that happen for the Minister, but also facilitated the recruitment of a known associate of the Minister in the place of the terminated public servant. Did you learn nothing from that shameful episode?

It is looking more and more like the concept of integrity in government is dying if not dead. One of your colleagues (likely another one 'too busy' to attend the Machinery of Government offered at the start of your Term) has come out in the media suggesting that Ministers probably should have *more* say in the hiring and firing of senior public servants, which of course would only serve to make public servants more politicised and subservient.

I have witnessed Ministers in the past who surrounded themselves with cronies, and subservient 'yes' men and women, it never ended well. I recall watching a particularly intelligent and savvy person with the title 'Senior Political

Adviser'(who had been headhunted from overseas by the Minister for those exact abilities) being berated by that Minister for daring to give the Minister their honest opinion. I was in the room, and it is still scorched into my memory.

To this day I still cringe when I think about it. Utterly pointless to "have a dog and bark yourself" as the saying goes. This particular Minister was known for their over inflated sense of competence and appalling decision making and was the *worst* person to be refusing sound advice! Much better in their position to surround themselves with 'old war-horses' and naysayers that spoke candidly to them and helped them avoid potential pitfalls.

To ignore that kind of sage advice just invites schadenfreude from the very people there to support you. On this basis alone politicians should be insisting on political neutrality from the public service – not just when they are the Opposition and no longer wield power over us.

I *truly* hope you take this opportunity to publicly state the importance of a return to true integrity in Hooseland, history has a long memory and you do want to be on the right side of it don't you?

Yours in service to the public,

Amber Guette (she/her)

The Mountain

Dear Minister

Suitably cold and miserable outside today and it definitely feels like our department is in the depths of winter... I want to address the political elephant in the room this month, your election promise of brand-new state-of-the-art community health centres in every town in Hooseland by your third year in government.

We are now two months past that deadline and things are looking pretty dire, but then it was never going to happen as those deadlines were arbitrary and not backed up by any evidence.

We knew when it was announced in opposition by your party (as one of several overly ambitious election promises dangled in front of the public to entice them to vote for you, I might add...) that it was madness to make such a promise. What groundwork had you done to see if it was even possible!? The sad thing is that as you now start to publicly back away from this 'flagship' policy, we are finally making progress and on track to achieve most, if not all, of what you promised Hooselanders in the next 3-5 years.

This is not an isolated problem, and so therefore should have been on your radar from the start. Around the world, governments often fail at implementing policy and public service projects.

As soon as I saw the Hooseland Government lowering the bar for the quality and size of clinics for delivery, I knew this would become just another pipe dream, failing to deliver what was promised to Hooselanders. But when the gerrymandering of how the health system recognises the boundaries of provinces started being used to cook the books, so that there are less "provinces" and therefore less clinics needed, I was ashamed to be a part of this project.

There is no need for this – I know we would never have made it to the full number promised, or within the promised timeframes, but we were making *progress* and the results, if this had remained a priority, would in the long-term have been a game changer for the health of Hooselanders. And now, bit by bit, and just as the public service is playing catch up on this you have decided to undermine it, why?

As I noted before it is no secret that globally there is a consistent pattern of failure in ambitious government project implementation. Those of us in the department tasked with making this promise a reality have been mulling over why we keep embarking on these election promises built on faulty logic with a disregard for the many moving parts and time required to do these ambitious projects properly. And this is not one sided, we are quite capable of coming up with ideas ourselves that have not had due policy consideration, for example, forging ahead with the operational work without considering the potential impacts on legislative settings that likely needed to change for a project to be a success.

It is a rare thing for the Ombudsman to call-out a government project failure as being an "unfathomable litany of errors" but there it is. So maybe it's time to better understand the 'why' of this kind of failure and how it can be avoided in future.

First and foremost, we all understand that new governments bring new ideas as they try and outbid each other in the elections for the hearts and minds (i.e., votes) of the public. Great – innovation – love it! But when new governments meet with public officials, that nod and blindly say yes, we can do that (all along knowing full well that it is not physically possible to achieve in the announced time-frame – and when questioned on it later give the lame excuse that 'but the Minister seemed so happy' !?!!!) we become equally culpable. This is quite literally setting us all up to fail!

Do you now understand better the letter I sent on why you need 'free and frank without fear or favour' advice? That the careers of public servants should not be at your whim, keeping our TOTP's on a short leash with fixed term contracts? The ability to provide that independent advice is at the heart of the integrity of the public service and is *crucial* to our role. It is how we best serve the Government of the day, and therefore, the Hooseland public.

Too often it seems that governments equate announcement with accomplishment. Again, Utopia is a great watch to see Ministers and officials thinking that just cutting the ribbon or turning up for a photo opportunity is enough.

Just as with our community health centres project – getting lots of attention from you and our *TOTP*'s at first, but as soon as it becomes the daily grind of the actual work (or worse, you finally acknowledge that what was promised can never be delivered on time) you all lose interest and start looking for the next shiny new project. All the work gets shunted down the line – from you to an associate Minister and down from the TOTP in CHAOS to some other inconsequential Higher-ups.

All of this is not helped by the fact that we have had multiple changes in Higher-up's over the course of the project, as the original champions of the project become burnt out and have resigned (taking all their knowledge of the conversations with your office with them). The new ones seem to all make the mistake of 'assuming' that the previous leader in that role had advised your office of the problems we are facing verbally (as certainly nothing has ever been allowed to be put in writing!)

This tends to leave well-intentioned, but totally inexperienced, public servants to respond to urgent issues on the project, cocking that up and then eventually joining their predecessor in resigning from the role. This kind of churn is a big part of the problem and why a record of everything sent/said to your office needs to be on the public record.

This lack of transparency over the lifetime of a project does not happen overnight – I have watched the disconnect in advice going to your office on the progress of the project. Bad news being sent to your office seems to be non-existent. All issues get minimised so that the red flags that should be alerting you to the issues are never up the flagpole so to speak. And lord help any of us that try to escalate the issues – if we speak up we are either ignored or worse, punished for the attempt to alert your office.

Right, well bearing that in mind I am henceforth alerting you to the fact that I have discovered discrepancies in the allocation of funding to some of the projects that those of us on the frontlines just cannot make sense of. Again, I tried to raise it with my Higher-up and got completely shut down and asked if I would be happier working in a different unit (this kind of not particularly veiled threat is increasingly more common sadly).

But have no fear, I intend to keep digging and get to the bottom of this – that much I can promise you. If corruption is going on at CHAOS it would have terrible implications for the Government, and for you as the Minister leading our department.

While I do not agree with everything you have done, you do not deserve to be tarnished with the ineptitude of public servants stuck in a role like a suit two sizes too big for them (hopefully it *is* just ineptitude, as I am pretty sure our integrity systems in CHAOS rule out corruption).

Yours in service to the public,

Amber Guette

Amber Guette (she/her)

Gimme Some Truth

Dear Minister

Been a busy week, hasn't it? With all the fuss in the media and question time in the House about *you know what*. We both know that all that could have been avoided with a wee bit of old-fashioned honesty when you first made that announcement based on figures that were wrong because *your* office had conflated two very different bits of departmental information and come to the wrong conclusion (despite, it turns out, having plenty of time to have it fact checked by us). And of course, instead of taking steps to correct the record due to 'human error', your people now insist we keep up the farce and make it true in retrospect!

So, of course six months later all hell breaks loose after our department wasted months on trying to make what you said correct in retrospect and the Opposition have used APFIA to work out the facts of what was said. All because of risk averseness to the truth – and a failure to admit what was initially a very minor cock up. Apart from the appalling waste of taxpayer's resources, the biggest loss in this was the opportunity to show leadership on integrity, something that could have been a game changer.

When will politicians learn that that the public LOVE it when a politician stuffs up and publicly admits it!? This sort of behaviour disproves the theory that politicians are not to be trusted and are lying bastards, who's only outstanding achievement is continuously winning the least trusted profession surveys in Hooseland.

I want to quote to you from the excellent television series Chernobyl, where a public servant, Valery Legasov gives us a soliloquy on the danger of lies: "What is the cost of lies? It's not that we'll mistake them for the truth. The real danger is that if we hear enough lies, then we no longer recognise the truth at all. What can we do then? What else is left but to abandon even the hope of truth and content ourselves instead with stories? In these stories, it doesn't matter who the heroes are. All we want to know is: 'Who is to blame?'"

Sorry to be so grumpy, but I predicted this escalating out of control at the start – not because I have amazing powers of prediction, but because I have seen it so many times in different governments and different departments. I know this can be a foreign concept in politics, but honesty really is the best policy in these shituations (no spellcheck – not a typo). I hope your people realise it is nearly impossible, thanks to our superb record keeping at CHAOS (you are welcome) to hide this kind of thing in the long term.

I know that back then the whole 'first 100 days in power' nonsense created an intense pressure to make fast progress in a naturally risk averse climate, but this inability to be honest on something minor really added to public servant visits to their GP for anxiety meds.

So please, in future let's agree to fact check before announcing and if things are said in error, PLEASE can we just rip that plaster off pronto and admit it? Much better than the slowly putrefying flesh-eating disease it grows into over time, followed by a media circus when it is discovered that you (well, your political advisor's but you carry the can for it) misled the House.

It is this atmosphere of risk averseness that makes it so hard for us to fully embrace all the good things, like breaking down silos, maintaining transparent and high integrity public service, and not wasting the public money on wild goose chases. You are better than this.

Okay, rant over – my frustration is getting the better of me, but sometimes I just feel like my head will explode when a lack of ownership turns the completely avoidable into a major pain in the neck.

On that topic I feel I need to alert you to what seems like some very odd goings on in CHAOS. I was, as I promised in my last letter, digging into what was going on with the discrepancies in the allocation of funding I found for the building of the new community health clinics in areas that had been identified by the department as being low need.

Not only that, but all my access to the information on the consortium's that have secured government funding for these projects has been pulled. That might stop any normal public servant but not me! I realised that I was not going to get anywhere by asking my Higher-up given the response I got last time, so I called in a favour from Steve in IT (he always seems to forget his lunch...) and he pulled the docs I needed from the server (apparently he had High Level Security access granted 10 years ago for a project and it never got revoked, so IT's slackness went in my favour for once!).

I have started going over the files we pulled, and one thing is really starting to stand out, all the building companies that have contracts for this work have different names, but I checked the Companies Office records, and they all have the same PO Box number!? I am just getting going so nothing other than that to report just yet but will let you know next month if I find anything that justifies my paranoia.

I just don't see how anything too dodgy could get past our integrity systems for procurement, so it is bound to be a storm in a teacup. I am pretty worn out with all these extra curricula activities on top of the normal workload so a shorter letter this month, I definitely need some sleep as my imagination is getting carried away working out possible reasons for the same PO Box.

Yours in service to the public,

Amber Guette (she/her)

Devil You Know

Dear Minister

It may sound crazy given all my concerns about this Government, but my biggest one continues to be that it fails. Why? Because I know no matter how much you personally stuff things up, one term for a government is just damaging to progress being made by public servants and economically bad for the public. It will mean the dismantling of all the policy work that has just started to bear fruit in Hooseland. If you lose the next election, it means at least another four years of waiting for real improvements in healthcare, education, welfare, infrastructure, etc.

So why would I want to risk that by holding your feet to the fire? Sure, it looks like you are doing bad things, but not as bad as them, right?

Well maybe I am tired of making excuses for always accepting the lesser of two evils, maybe I want what's right and good for Hooselanders? I know I sound like a broken record, but I had such hope for this Government – but all the heights I had hoped you would reach kept falling too far short of what you could have done for Hooseland – so shame on you.

Not having an opportunity to govern and being in opposition for so long has made you craven for keeping power by keeping the conservatives, (who only voted for you out of desperation for change in their own complacent party) happy. They are *not* your base, but your base is losing faith rapidly because you have never given them what they needed – and more importantly, what you promised.

Watching you govern is increasingly like going for an eye exam – you know, when they keep changing the lenses on you and asking repeatedly – better or worse? Better or worse? And the closer you get to seeing clearly the harder it is to tell, but you feel like you have to pick one, right? Is it better or worse or same-same? Increasingly Hooselanders face a similar choice between your lot, and the conservative party.

So, my dilemma is, do I continue to demand better of your Government or do I have to settle for the lesser of two evils? Last year, according to polling by the Hooseland Clarion, only a *quarter* of Hooselanders said they trusted "people in government", down from 57% in 2013 (which to be honest was still pretty shocking IMO). On those numbers it is pretty clear that if voting wasn't compulsory in Hooseland, voter turnout would be plummeting.

As a 'progressive' government you are expected to be able to make tough decisions and make them quickly. If you procrastinate for a week, you will simply have another whole set of problems come up that you have to make a decision on. The public service will support you – yes, we will give you all the pros and cons, but once you have decided we *will* support you.

Your job is to listen to conflicting advice and make a judgement call to the best of your knowledge in the best interest of the public. Of course, you will make mistakes – 20/20 hindsight is always the best, but it is still better than doing nothing and being so risk averse that no progress is ever made.

Look, as a rule Hooselanders tend to find the Opposition leader cringe-inducing. They have been caught lying and bullying members of their own party! And yet, due to their decisive nature, they are still currently polling higher than our PM! Historically, while your parties' manifesto has never been that inspiring, it has been the passionate way in which its modernising promise was articulated after eight years of conservative government that excited and energised voters. Where has that energy gone?

More than ever what Hooseland needs is for you to admit the errors that have been made (the public tend to be forgiving of stuff ups as they can relate being human themselves) and to commit to moving forward with more accountable government, progressive evidence-based policy, and improvements in democratic accountability.

They wanted a government that would heal the decades old wounds of division (the ones that the Opposition are busily working on cracking open and sprinkling salt on by using issues like the rights of indigenous people and those on welfare as levers). A platform of national unity is needed now more than ever in Hooseland.

On a different, but related topic I was dismayed to see you requesting information this close to the elections that, given the content, was clearly for electioneering purposes. That was bad enough, but I was even more dismayed to see that no one in CHAOS thought to push back on the request! Your Political Advisor even says in their request "I understand this is to be used for a speech at an industry luncheon this week...."

While I doubt that your political advisors bother to familiarise themselves with public service rules and regulations, guidance from the Hooseland Public Service Commission is clear: "In the pre-election period Ministers should not request policy work to support their party-political, for example, to use in election campaign debates. Public servants who are concerned they are being asked to work on something that is not part of the government policy process, should inform their chief executive". Yeah, right, like that is going to happen in the current TOTP 'give them anything they want' climate.

And before CHAOS even gets involved in responding to these sorts of requests (especially those being made by political advisors from the Ministers office) then our Ministerial Unit should be involved, and guidance sought from the likes of a Principal Advisor about the appropriateness of information requests. If necessary, clarity over the request should, at the very least, be sought!

Your lot need to remember that you have only had one term and that is never enough to be complacent – yes, the election is yours to lose, but remember that Stockholm syndrome is real and Hooselanders have had many more years of the Opposition in power – and this can have a big effect on the national psyche – creating a culture of 'learnt helplessness' and acceptance that a bullying government is a strong one, and may even be preferable to a 'soft government' and deep down perhaps even suspecting it is all no better than they deserve.

Yours in service to the public,

Amber Guette

Amber Guette (she/her)

Dirty Work

Dear Minister

What are your memories of your first job? The first job I had as a graduate from university in the public service in the Injury Compensation Department of the Hooseland Public Service.

I was a claims officer for dental injuries, and I will never forget the crap they expected us to do and the number of valid claims they made us deny was just awful. I was continuously getting told off for letting too many claims through. The final straw for me was the day when I was yelled at by my Higher-up for not declining the claim of a woman who had been the victim of domestic abuse and had lost her front teeth in an attack by her partner. I was told all the things I could have said to deny the claim (not the least that it wasn't technically an accident as her partner had intended to do the harm he did). I quit on the spot and travelled overseas working as I went for minimum wage, but at least I could sleep at night.

And now here I am, many decades on having served loyally as a servant of the public ever since I returned from my two years in the wilderness. Once again not being able to sleep at night because of what I know and the part I am supposed to play in it all. I will explain what that is shortly, but first I want to share a couple of stories that will set the scene for mine.

The first one was told to me by a Senior Advisor in government Comms. They had just joined a new department and were asked by their colleague to attend a meeting that the TOTP was holding. This particular TOTP was so domineering that they were warned not to say *anything* at all, *no matter what was said*. They thought this very odd but had no reason not to trust their new colleague. It turned out that all of the senior 'leadersheep' team (SLT) were there, and despite the fact that they all knew that what the TOTP said they were going to do would be a complete disaster media wise, not one of them said a thing. At the last minute the TOTP realised themselves after saying it out loud that it would do more harm than good, and in the end backed away from it. All the while the SLT just sat nodding in agreement – *no one* in that organisation was willing to contradict the TOTP, even at great risk to the organisation and the TOTP themselves.

The second story is one I witnessed first-hand. A Higher-up was telling a Comms Advisor what to put in a media release – the Comms Advisor did what they were paid to do and advised the Higher-up that it would not be advisable to send that message at that particular time and for their efforts got abused publicly by the Higher-up, who screamed at them that they were just a "lowly fucking wet behind the ears advisor" and to just "do what I fucking say!"

Cleverly, the Comms Advisor sent the draft media release to the Minister's office (as part of the whole no-surprises approach of course) which resulted in an angry call from them telling the Higher-up to "pull it immediately".

The Comms Advisor knew they would get a bollocking for sharing this but did the right thing anyway (and had the smarts to start looking for work elsewhere knowing full well that the Higher-up would be slow to forgive – even though it would have been worse for the Higher-up had it been released...).

So, you must be wondering why I am sharing these stories with you now? The first was to illustrate how those that refuse to listen risk a room full of nodding heads that will let them do the wrong thing out of fear, rather than act with integrity. The second story is to show you the reason I serve the public, to be like that Comms Advisor, to do the right thing no matter the consequences, because I know the public good far outweighs my career.

Okay so I am not completely naive, it is a matter of public record that there have been instances of corruption in the Hooseland Public Service, and I attended a procurement conference once where one of the speakers asked all the attendees (a mix of private and public sector procurement specialists) to close their eyes and raise their hand if they had witnessed corruption in their workplace in the last three years.

Once the exercise was done the speaker informed us that about 80% of the room had raised their hand. Some may have suspected that it may have been an exaggeration on the behalf of the speaker in order to shock us into thinking harder about our integrity systems, but I *may* have sneaked a peek so I can confirm that was correct. At the time as a non-hand raiser, I felt a bit left out, but I sadly suspect I am about to join the ranks of the hand-raisers.

The Hooseland Independent Commission against Corruption (HICAC) was established in 1989 (the 80's were heady times for corruption) to respond to allegations in the House about the integrity of our public service. They investigated allegations of fraud, nepotism, bribery, improper allocation of contracts, unauthorised secondary employment and failure to declare conflicts of interest.

We are all aware of the investigation that exposed an extraordinary example of this at RailCom. If you are not familiar with it already, I recommend looking it up – a salutary lesson in reaping what you sow.

The litany of corruption that was exposed is horrific, from building self-storage complexes for private purposes with RailCom funds, trading sexual favours for government subsidised cartage agreements and certain individuals getting promotions by bribery, it would appear that the Hooseland Public Service is a place where corruption cannot only happen, but given the right circumstances flourishes! This is not the public service that most Hooselanders would hope for.

Now back to why I no longer sleep at night. I know I am getting closer to the truth because I am being blocked at every turn. Access to items I never had any issue accessing has mysteriously disappeared.

Instead, I had a request from my Higher-up to use some of the leave I have outstanding due to "HR" issues. What issues!? I can promise you that none of this will put me off my search for the truth on this matter. I am beginning to understand why we have a mismatch in where the new health clinics are being approved to be built versus our policy work and research outcomes on the areas of highest need.

I hate to even say this out loud Minister, but I suspect corruption! Yes, corruption – in CHAOS! This is a sad position to find myself in, I mean I know corruption exists, but I have never seen any in practice and had hoped that would remain my experience.

Last week I spoke to a colleague (one of the Higher-ups that has real integrity) and they told me they had been in a meeting with you and that you had requested that their advice and the conversation not be recorded (strike one for you in my opinion I should add).

They told me they had gone to that meeting to have a robust discussion with you and your office on the anomalies they had uncovered in the project. This record of the discussion is not a 'nice to have' you understand. There are obligations on us in the Hooseland Public Service under our Public Records Act to have full and accurate records and to document the key outcomes and decisions from these conversations. These records are crucial for institutional knowledge and not doing so breaches the trust of the Hooseland public on our ability to maintain transparent government.

How can you not understand the slippery slope you create when you put a public servant in the awkward situation of choosing to either refuse your request or ignore their role as servants of the public in keeping accurate records? As a public leader you need to understand that the rot starts at the top. The way you behave towards public servants can translate into them behaving like that to their subordinates and so on and so on, until the public rightly believe we are all corrupt. Leadership is everything Minister.

Your lack of willingness to have conversations on the record about the anomalies we are uncovering is forcing me to consider that you know more about what has been happening regarding the placement of the new health clinics in areas that appear to be more aligned with certain 'friends' of your Government than the genuine need of Hooselanders.

For the first time I need to say that I am seriously doubting my role as a servant of the people under your Government. It was bad enough under the previous lot having to justify my work as a public servant being to 'keep the bastards honest', but to start to doubt a Government I had such high hopes for is quite devastating.

For my part I don't want to see our department enter

the annals of history as one of the corrupt ones, but I am staying to continue to try and uncover the truth.

Yours in service to the public,

Amber Guette

Amber Guette (she/her)

Bewitched, Bothered and Bewildered

Dear Minister

Do you remember what it was like at the early stages of a romance or a crush? When the person who had captured your heart seemed like perfection – you could find no fault in them. Well, that is how I saw you when you came to power nearly four years ago. You seemed so shiny and bright, with a skip in your step and a very genuine smile and determination to bring light to the lives of Hooselanders – you seemed to me to be the essence of integrity.

Back then I too regained the skip in my step and the hope that my dreams of a more equal Hooseland, that recognised that 'trickle-down theory' was a scam created by those who wanted to be at the top of the pyramid with the power to decide what parts of our nation got the 'trickle' of resources and funding, and what parts suffered from perpetual drought.

I thought – at last! Someone in power who really wants to make a difference – I was, as this month's song says, quite bewitched by that prospect. But like most relationships that start out with wide eyed optimism the cracks have been showing for quite a while now, and I am well into the bothered and bewildered phase of our relationship.

At first it was just the glacial speed with which things seemed to be happening, and the ignoring of advice from our department, but it has gone way past that now – what seemed to be incompetence, and perhaps being new to the job, and not yet fully understanding your role, has blossomed into full blown conspiracy level bullshit!

You said at the start of your term as a Minister in Hooseland that you wanted a public service that was free and frank – well, here it is – this Government has well and truly lost its shine – and so have you. Now I understand why you let the State Services Department remove the Hooseland Public Service Integrity and Behaviour Internal Audit.

This annual anonymous check-in with the public service on our thoughts on integrity, leadership and how well we were doing our job was invaluable for getting to the heart of matters. It was the one chance to *really* give our free and frank opinion without fear or favour on our workplace. The results were always eagerly awaited by those of us who are committed to seeing improvements in our public service. Was it the increasingly bad reports that the TOTP were getting from public servants? Or was it the increasing reports of seeing behaviour such as conflicts of interest or bullying that persuaded your Government that this was not the kind of honesty you wanted from us?

We were able to gain incredibly valid data and show concerning trends from the continuity of this survey annually. All pointing to the areas where we needed to try harder, to improve our score as a public service. Well, you may have done away with that tool, but you cannot keep us quiet.

It was done with a heavy heart, but I could no longer turn a blind eye to what I am seeing here at CHAOS, I have had no option but to escalate my concerns to a Higher-up that I trust in another team in CHAOS. Clearly my one is ignoring my frequently voiced concerns, but it is high time an investigation into corruption on our flagship health centre project was undertaken.

I am sad to say some of the evidence I have seen now very clearly points to your office being implicated in this, and it seems to go deep into higher levels of the Hooseland Public Service as well. At first, I tried to rationalise what I was seeing, but now it cannot be unseen. I could have explained away the odd red flag (and trust me I wanted to be able to very badly), but not anymore....

I read the article in the Hooseland Clarion last weekend that you and some of your colleagues had contributed to, boohooing about how hard it is to be a Minister and complaining about public servants having the home ground, and that you were seen as a 'visitor' by us. That it is 'natural' to feel suspicious of the advice public servants are providing, after all, they have just been serving the rival political party for eight years.

Well, dear Minister, that is a two-way street, and it takes time to establish trust. I saw complaints from one of your colleagues about how they had "had no training beforehand, no training after, no support after and a massive Briefing to the incoming Minister document prepared by the department which they never got time to read". Seriously? If that is what you believe too then please go back to my Truth and Freedom letter in that first few months – most don't even take up the training they are offered! So cry me a river.

While I agree that most of the work Ministers do is unseen by the public (responding to constituents' requests, signing out mountains of correspondence, responding to Briefings and ploughing through legislative paperwork), this applies equally to our work as public servants. But none of that is any excuse for how you and some of my colleagues have behaved.

I am sad because you had such an opportunity to do the

right thing and instead you chose the other path, using your power for your own devices, and that has now turned my sadness to anger.

You say your job is 'hard and demanding'? Well think of all the poor Hooseland taxpayers at their hard and demanding jobs, in much less comfortable environments than yours, paying for you to abuse their trust and not deliver the health clinics they were promised four years ago.

I stupidly had put all my faith in our implicit integrity systems to prevent something like this happening, but clearly there is nothing stopping these being ignored. I am now having to trust that a brave Higher-up outside of the project will ensure that this gets the proper attention it demands and put an end to the dodgy deals being done. It is still not too late for you to fix this for Hooseland, but you will have to own this publicly, resign and have your Government promise it will all be put right and that Hooselanders will get what they were promised all along.

Yours in service to the public,

Amber Guette (she/her)

What's In It for You?

Dear Minister

Clearly, I have been wasting my breath trying to convince you to fix the mess that has been created on your watch.

I want to note for the record that having the Higher-up I trusted to ensure this got looked into properly promoted to another city was a slick move, and that getting me shunted to another team in our department with zero input on the project was a good attempt to shut me down, but I am not going away that easily.

I have been following the notices in the Hooseland Clarion and there continues to be major irregularities in the areas getting kept in the 'green for go' pile of new Community Health Centres. I have been mapping them alongside the areas of highest need and there continues to be no correlation. There *is* however a correlation with areas that the largest political donations to your party in the public register have come from, coincidence? I think not.

You see I have been privy to all the successive Briefings we have sent you on this and have seen what has come back from your office, seen the handwritten notations, the bits circled on our recommendations where you have disagreed with what was proposed. I watched as each time the Briefings went across to your office, they came closer to reflecting the current state.

I saw the looks of consternation and worry on the Programme Lead and the Principal Adviser as they read what had come back from your office and heard the raised voices between the Higher-ups and them that led eventually to one of them resigning and one being transferred to another department, signalling yet another blow to the integrity of the Hooseland Public Service.

And who now is left to ask the difficult questions? They have replaced us all of course; with widgets they know will not cause problems by looking too closely or asking any difficult questions – because the widgets are smart enough to know that is not the way careers are made in the Hooseland Public Service....

What I really want to know Minister is – why?! You are paid a good salary; your party has plenty of grassroots support? Do you really think the money is worth it!? Did you have such a low opinion of the public service that you thought no one would challenge you? What did you offer them to buy their silence? Bigger and better career opportunities? Surely you can't *always* have thought this way, but golly, if you did you missed your calling, as you would be very well suited to a career in acting.

Given how stringent vetting is for public servants, I'm genuinely interested to know why it is not stricter for our Ministers? Knowing what I know now about how questionable and clearly at times criminal, Ministers can be, I think this needs a harder look. It's kind of an awkward situation when you think about it, the idea that people can elect whoever they want to serve them, with no background checks or standards to meet. If they want to elect a lying, corrupt charlatan as a Minister there is nothing to prevent them.

How do we Hooselanders vet our potential candidates to ensure they are not there to take advantage of the public by influence peddling, bribery, nepotism, extortion, misappropriation of taxpayer's money, etc....

Opportunity wise there are many ways a Minister can

exercise corruption. But I ask you why risk a potentially very rewarding career where you can be seen as a hero or at least as on the right side of history, and instead dedicate yourself to disobeying Hooseland's integrity systems and ethical standards to benefit yourself and your cronies?

Perhaps you don't really understand yourself? I did some research, mostly to satisfy my own curiosity, but now that I have done it, I may as well share it with you. Psychology, sociology, administration theory, history and economics provide us some explanations.

Studies have shown that corruption is more common in environments which encourage it, and less common in situations where there are stricter controls. Well, that makes sense, but that excuse cannot be given in your case, as the Hooseland Public Service had a pretty good reputation for integrity and has often topped the charts for it globally in indexes.

Now we have all heard the saying that power corrupts, but it turns out this is not necessarily true! Studies show that politicians are rarely corrupt by themselves. Instead, they tend to act in groups, which not only collaborate, but make the illegal action seem righteous and acceptable, (this would explain the way you have worked with senior public servants to gain your dodgy ends).

Also, just saying 'power corrupts' does not explain why it doesn't *always* corrupt – plenty of people in power can rise above corruption and do the right thing. So, power does *not* corrupt; but it can act like a lens and magnify an individual's moral tendencies. I guess that has the finger pointed right back at you.

I have argued many times in the workplace that we need to make our integrity systems in Hooseland less *implicit* and seen as a high trust environment that relies on the good will of individuals, but more *explicit* and have integrity systems put in place that would make it very difficult for corrupt activity to occur.

That and actually encouraging whistleblowing and creating a culture where people felt they could raise issues safely and early if they spotted them. This is about culture change at the very heart of public service. It may help the independence of the public service, as well as remove a temptation from Ministers, if they did not have so much power over the hiring and firing of the roles too!

I have learnt the hard way that sometimes, Higher-ups and TOTP's will not always offer you leadership or guidance, but just look at you with blank stares when you have the courage to tell them what is happening at the coalface. All that is going through their minds is what does this mean for me and my career – not their staff or the department or the public.

And that, dear Minister is why you have gotten away with what you have done. Because it did not just come down to what was in it for you, but what there was in it for many others who could have stopped you but chose not to.

Yours in service to the public,

Amber Guette (she/her)

Whistleblower

Dear Minister

So, by now you know that it was me that blew the whistle to the Hooseland Clarion. Of course you know – who else could it be? I was the only one who knew enough to point out where the bodies are buried. You thought you had it all sown up, that everyone you could bribe with offers of greater glory (and pay) to be a part of this fiasco had been, and that the rest would be too scared to do anything about it for fear of losing the golden handcuffs of a safe career in the Hooseland Public Service right?

Wrong. I Amber Eslanda Guette could not stand by and watch a major corruption scandal take place in CHAOS. Not after I had seen the evidence of the payments being made to your political party by vested interests for the placement of the new state-of-the-art public health clinics in areas of value to them, and the backhanders from construction monopoly's that got the contracts to build them. So yes, I went to the media with all the information I have been quietly keeping a copy of over the last year.

As you are aware, this was not my first choice – I tried escalating to my Higher-up and would have gone to the TOTP if I had not already seen that they were a part of the corruption too. I tried to pull in another Higher-up, but you corrupted them, and gave them a promotion they would never normally have seen in their lifetime, in a department far away from your portfolio of interests.

Once I realised that I was blocked at every point that I

turned to, you left me with only two choices, stay silent and feel the shame of letting down the Hooseland public and let you win, or take a dangerous stand and go to the Media.

In my head there was no choice. I am a servant of the public like my parents before me, I am like Horton the elephant (with the longest memory) who had heard the tiny call of the Hooselanders that had no oversight over what was happening and who, as always, would be the ones to lose.

The Hooseland Clarion have been amazing (despite all the slagging off the Media have had over the past decade) and have kept my identity a secret, even with the full wrath of the Government coming down upon them. They are heroes. But you know and I know it was me, and if you choose to out me, then so be it.

I have no regrets and would do the same thing again if I had to. However, the election is coming up in just four months, and outing me would just put you and your Government even more firmly in the spotlight – so let's just say that you have considerations too.

I have had time to reflect on why Hooseland has a reputation for being transparent and free from corruption – I mean how true is this really? Is it just that internationally the bar is pretty low, or do we need to rethink how we define corruption and the climate that is needed for it to flourish in first world nations?

I have had to think long and hard about my role as a public servant, and in the end my responsibility to ensure that I was holding the line won out. If things that were wrong came to my attention, then the buck had to stop there. It was up to me, no one else, to take the stewardship we are charged with as servants of the people and prove to them that some public servants valued our integrity as public servants more than their own career prospects.

If the public are to take us seriously, then we need to prove that we are capable of integrity, capable of advising future ministers and governments no matter the cost to ourselves. As public servants we have an obligation to think about the long term as well as the present, implications of our behaviour, that is our stewardship responsibility.

What happens to us Hooseland whistleblowers? I asked my union this previously and they admitted they did not know. Public servants who risk their careers to expose deception and misconduct are true Hooseland patriots, but no one can tell me what the future likely holds because no one valued it enough to find out. My earlier letter 'Honesty' touched on your plans to make retaliation against whistleblowers illegal, interestingly that never got passed in the House, I guess now I know why.

Let's be honest about one thing at least – there is no freedom of speech in the Hooseland Public Service. Our contracts as public servants stand as the greatest oppression of free speech in this nation. In a truly free Hooseland there would not be any restrictions on the speech of any individual permitted outside of work. There is no room for whistleblowers in our society.

The gagging of not just public servants, but NGOs, and indeed anyone accessing public funding (as some beneficiaries have learnt the hard way when they bravely dared to speak publicly about government policy) that is at the heart of what is wrong with the system.

Politicisation has been a growing problem in the public service for many years now, there have been concerns that officials working in government agencies have become far too subservient to government ministers (a point you once made in opposition).

This is the 'politicisation' of the public service – because public servants are expected to serve the Minister's political edicts without question, rather than the wider interests of the public. This has led to the widely held view, including among many of us public servants, that in the past couple of decades we have been pushed into focusing too much on serving ministers, even to the point of *anticipating* what their Ministers might want to hear (and at the risk of getting this very wrong).

I have personally witnessed a Hooseland TOTP urging public servants to escalate an ever-growing budget blow-out in relation to an event a Minister was holding, even though doing so was a genuine risk to that Minister if it made it on to the front page of the Hooseland Clarion.

Political neutrality and trustworthiness *must* be bottom lines for the Hooseland Public Service. The matters that I raised at CHAOS go to the heart of trust and confidence in a key public service agency. Cases like mine raise questions about the rigour of our integrity systems, and about whether individuals can or should speak up, even if the wider organisation or agency has signed off on a course of action. Your serve.

Yours in service to the public,

Amber Guette

Amber Guette (she/her)

Titanium

Dear Minister

Well, I did say 'your serve' in closing last month's letter so I should not be surprised to find that serve you did and that I was made redundant from CHAOS a week later. Good move though, keeping it out of the media, I guess you had no need of that when you have the CHAOS TOTP so firmly in your pocket (or should that be wallet?).

You will be pleased to know that being torn from my beloved public service left me (albeit temporarily) broken, and very depressed. However, I refuse to let you win – I intend to keep going and not walk away from the dumpster fire that this country's government is becoming.

Your coalition partner the Enviro Party intelligently distanced themselves from your attempts to downplay your corruption of the public service and demanded a full investigation into what they recognised as a major integrity failing on behalf of the Government they had signed up to support.

I am also very happy to say that one of their political advisors sought me out and thanked me for my service in whistleblowing on their Coalition partners lack of integrity.

They have put their money where their mouth is and have taken me on as a researcher on whistleblowing in their research unit after I 'lost' my job at CHAOS. They quite literally saved me from drowning in self-pity and made me realise that I am stronger than either you or I thought I was.

I am very much enjoying the luxury of being paid to do

the research I was doing for free in my previous role. For example, did you know that by combing through the eight years of the Hooseland Public Service Integrity and Behaviour Internal Audit under the previous Government (no data on your Government as you conveniently cancelled it...)I have discovered the three most commonly observed negative behaviours were bullying (observed by 73%), conflicts of interest being ignored (55%) and abusive or intimidating behaviour (43%), up over the last eight years from 33%, 19% and 29% respectively. These dramatic results in relation to the survey clearly show that no matter who is in power an effort needs to be made in the public service to increase our efforts to encourage public servants to speak out about wrongdoing, and for the Higher-ups and TOTP to ensure that swift and visible action is taken in response to such reports, and that public servants who do speak out are protected from negative consequences for fulfilling their responsibility to report. Fascinating – and the complete opposite of what happened to me of course.

The results prove that my experience was not an isolated one. I thought I was alone, but I guess that is what those perpetrating this level of dysfunction in our public service wanted me to think.

You would expect that research like this should have been done long ago in order to ensure continuous improvements in the Hooseland Public Service, but it took a minority political party to make this a priority. We can no longer rely on the bravery of public servants to report wrongdoing, or that when they do, there will be the political will to investigate and act on such clear breaches of integrity and conduct.

The Hooseland Public Service's historical reputation for integrity was hard won but is proving to be easily lost. As the old saying goes, you measure what you treasure, and the 'measuring' ended with the stopping of the Integrity and Behaviour Internal Audit.

Clearly sustaining and improving integrity requires strong leadership from the TOTP's and a government that values it. What is really unfair is that many of my colleagues in CHAOS have worked hard to establish best practice integrity and conduct, only to see it eroded by the selfish few who saw more reward in behaving corruptly to meet your ends, than protecting our reputation as a high integrity public service – so shame on them!

Most public servants want their image among Hooselander's to reflect their pride in their profession, but thanks to the rapidly dropping integrity standards, and scandals they instead have to listen to the increasing public servant bashing in the media (frequently from politicians who should know better).

This is resulting in a death spiral, as cumulative attacks on us lower our morale and willingness to fight the system from within, the good ones lose faith and leave to work in the private sector (often to face the same low integrity levels, but at least the pay is better, and they no longer have the high expectations they entered public service with).

To restore Hooseland's public servants' pride in our profession, we need to urgently address the drop in integrity standards and the bashing of public servants. Our *belief* in ourselves is inherently related to our ability to serve the public. Our research is highlighting the (bleeding obvious in my opinion) importance of ethical leadership from our Ministers and the TOTP.

The research's main conclusion is that the professional pride of Hooseland's public servants is at great risk currently. Combing through the interviews with fellow whistleblowers revealed the widespread use of vengeful tactics.

Of those that decided to stay in the public service after they outed corruption, a shocking 81 percent of them said they were marginalised and ignored when it came to promotions, (despite having done the 'right thing' according to our Code of Conduct). 79 percent of respondents said they faced counteraccusations, and 65 percent were devalued, receiving lower performance ratings and being denied promotions.

I saw reflected in their words my own experience with life after whistleblowing. The all telling symptoms of post-traumatic stress disorder, depression and suicidal tendencies, feelings of discouragement, hopelessness, unfairness and failure. Adding further distress, whistleblowers in the research material often had to fight to get their jobs back or be compensated for loss of employment etc.

This can all take *years* off the whistleblower's lives. Our colleagues see this of course, and that all has a chilling effect on those who have seen what we see but are too scared to speak up. I would like to say what doesn't kill you makes you stronger, and maybe one day I will be able to say that, but for now I just feel numb. I get up each day and go to work to uncover more and more reasons why whistleblowers need protection – not more protection or better protection – just any protection at all.

Yours in service to the public,

Amber Guette (she/her)

Dance Only with Me

Dear Minister

Well, the repercussions of the whistleblowing seem to have been pretty light for you so far considering. Your Government's spin doctors did an amazing job of making light of it and it did not hurt that you had some major TOTP's in the Hooseland Public Service who had everything to lose if it had blown up backing them up.

The only fallout seems to be that your coalition partner (and my current employer) the Enviro Party have stated that they are open to joining with other parties' post-election to form a government if the public decide they want a change of government at the polls. Good for them! I guess they are distancing themselves, which is fair enough under the circumstances.

Given that, I was amazed to see in the Hooseland Clarion front page yesterday that you are calling their so called "bluff" and deciding ahead of the election that you will no longer opt to form a coalition government with them in the face of what you are calling a lack of "loyalty"!

Wow – firstly, loyalty is for dogs and how 'loyal' have you proven to them – creating a scandal that could have bought them down as well as yourselves?? What arrogance – have you learned nothing – or did the light repercussions embolden you to think you have gotten away with it? To tell them they can make a coalition with you, and only you, does not bode well for the future of democratic leadership.

I am surprised the party faithful have not told you to get

over yourselves – there are greater things at risk here than your egos! The first (so called) progressive government we have had in ages, and you want to risk that because they would not support the spin that the "fraudulent behaviour was all a big misunderstanding, that was blown out of all proportion by the media..." (you can mentally insert the rolling eyes emoji here please and thank you).

The whole point of a coalition government is to represent a wider range of people and a bigger range of views, therefore making them more democratic and fairer. In countries where coalition governments are rare, there are often just two main parties who can form a government. At least in a coalition government voters might have a *chance* of voting for a party they really feel represents them. It's a bit like buying a house and thinking, well I might only be able to afford this kind of house in this slightly shitty neighbourhood, but at least I can paint and decorate it the way I like! Do you really want to take that choice away from Hooselanders?

It is not like you have many other suitable candidates for coalition – the PACT party are too far to the conservative/ anti-social responsibility side of the political compass to appeal to your base, and you have completely alienated the First Peoples Representatives Party by refusing to look seriously at the damage done (and still being done – the placement of the health clinics ringing any bells?) to the indigenous people of Hooseland.

It will be very interesting to see what the national political polls say next fortnight. I am not sure how *fond* of political polls Hooselanders are (or more to the point, the ways in which those polls are used by the media/politicians), but even if they are just a metaphorical 'licked finger in the air' trying to establish which way the political wind is blowing, most of us still believe that politicians should pay attention to them as one of the ways of hearing Hooselanders voices.

Let's be honest, unless it fits with your already established thinking, the connections between public opinion and government action can be called tenuous at best (as is illustrated by your Government's refusal to hold an enquiry into the corruption claims at CHAOS, despite polls showing that many Hooselanders think this would be a good idea).

And yet, adding to the incongruity, there is also a fear that politicians too often put their 'fingers to the wind of public opinion' in deciding what direction they should be seen to be heading in (personally from what I have seen, you are more preoccupied with what the Opposition think than the public).

Either way, ignoring the opportunity to regain the trust of both the Enviro Party and the Hooseland public is at your own peril, and despite your best efforts in manipulating the message on your corruption, you are starting to look more and more like a wallflower that no one wants to pick for the next dance.

Yours in service to the public,

Amber Guette (she/her)

Pass Me By

Dear Minister

Just wow – I thought it was bad enough that you were being so rude to your coalition partner, but now the public!? I was pleased to see that in tandem with the polling on likely voting preferences, a national poll looking at the appetite for introducing a referendum on greater transparency around party political funding was introduced.

And what do we get in response to that? Your Government saying that *when* you are re-elected (!?!) you will not support having a referendum (saying it is politically motivated by the Media) you seriously need to be reading the room on this one....

Meanwhile, two months out from the elections and you have not only lost your coalition partner, but due to your arrogance, and a refusal to meet the public on where they stand regarding political funding, you have had resoundingly low polling numbers. Assuming of course that they are accurate, opinion polls have a story to tell.

In this instance the story is that your Government would lose any election held today. Hooselanders clearly expect better from their politicians – integrity, transparency and honesty are top of mind, not that they will get that from the other front-runners, but then they do not necessarily expect that from them as it is not their 'brand', but it *was* supposed to be yours!

The polls are a clear message from Hooselanders that you cannot be trusted to govern alone, and that without the tension of a coalition partner to balance out your hubris, the lack of progress on urgent issues and the scandal of the corruption has finally turned the majority of Hooselanders against you. And you have no one to blame but yourselves – the power was yours to lose.

But what have you been doing? Blaming everyone else for the low polls – your disloyal coalition partner, the easily led public, the lying Opposition, the economy, even the bad results our national sporting teams have had lately... (seriously desperate) and the list goes on.

I want to share something with you I saw on the TV the other night, it made me think of you.... I have never watched it before but in trying to avoid news coverage of the latest depressing climate news I was flicking through the channels and came across this strange cartoon where the main character is a horse, but also a man, so a horse/man if that isn't too much of a stretch, called funnily enough BoJack Horseman. Anywho, as I said he reminded me of what you have become, so I went online and got a transcript of the bit I thought you really needed to hear, so here goes:

BoJack Horseman: It happened again. Why do I keep thinking things will make me happy. What is wrong with me?

Ana: BoJack, don't do this. Don't fetishize your own sadness.

BoJack: Uh.... Oh, god, I'm drowning. I feel like I'm drowning.

Todd: You can't keep doing this. You can't keep doing shitty things and then feel bad about yourself like that makes it okay. You need to be better.

BoJack: I know and I'm sorry. I was drunk there was all this pressure with the Oscar campaign but now... now that it's over....

Todd: No! No, BoJack, just stop. *You* are all the things that are wrong with you. It's not the alcohol or the drugs or any of the shitty things that happened to you in your career or when you were a kid. It's you. Alright, it's you. Fuck man, what else is there to say.

Well, there it is – I will just leave that there for you to consider, but I doubt you will see the similarities between Mr Horseman and yourself in time to save this election.

Like many politicians before you, once caught out you were 'sorry, not sorry'. You know, pretend sorry while blaming everyone else for your misfortunes rather than owning it. 'Sorry' that you had been 'too trusting' of those you were doing business with. 'Sorry' you hadn't seen the 'lack of stomach your coalition partners had for the realities of leadership'. The real tone of your response to anything that happened was 'it's not really fair to blame me for other people's failings'.

Your leader, our Prime Minister actually tried to use the argument that four years was not enough and that if Hooselanders really believed in fairness then you should really be given another four years! That elections should be done with a conservative mindset, not as a means of punishing the behaviour of a few bad apples.... A few bad apples!? This is starting to look more like a cider factory...! Telling the public what a 'fair' election is and is not sounds a lot like 'polisplaining' to Hooselanders – we will decide what a fair election is thank you very much.

Adding insult to injury, a text message from your Parties President critical of you surfaced last Sunday. The message stated that they always found you a "slippery character to deal with" and that they had "never fully trusted" you. This begs the question why they were willing to back someone as a Minister when they clearly did not trust you?

Despite your lack of willingness to take the need for a referendum on political party funding seriously, there is one referendum you cannot escape – the election in two months' time will effectively be a referendum on your party's ability to govern.

This whole debacle has been exhausting, Hooselanders do not deserve this, the vast majority of public servants do not deserve this (clearly the Matryoshka doll ones that supported your bad behaviour do, but none of us deserve them either).

Yours in service to the public,

Amber Guette

Amber Guette (she/her)

Is That All There Is?

Dear Minister

Yikes – three weeks out from going the election and it really is not looking good for your Government, is it? It actually physically *hurts* me to think that four years of hard work (not to mention taxpayers hard earned dollars) by public servants could all amount to a hill of beans as many of the progressive programmes that you promised the Hooseland public in the last election are about to go down the drain....

It is so deflating after the hope I felt four years ago – I look back on those earlier letters I sent you and have to ask where did she go? The optimistic naive public servant that thought communication was the key to fixing everything.

And now due to the failure of your Government to deliver with integrity, *we* are faced with losing all the ground we had started to gain in the health sector thanks to a fatal flaw in our governance system, major public sector projects that are already underway will be scuppered just because the new government didn't dream them up.

Incoming Hooseland governments should have to make a case that includes the financial and social cost if they want to end major government projects.

In recent years, there have been widespread concerns about the lack of capability in the government, and its failure to meet important public goals. The struggle to deliver solutions to crucial public challenges, such as tackling greenhouse gas emissions or reducing child poverty rates (the highest in the developed world), has seen trust in the

Hooseland Government at an all-time low.

You probably think how can that be? The previous government not only did nothing to fix these problems, it actively exacerbated them with its greedy corporate model of governance – but it all comes down to expectations, you can't be disappointed by something you never had hope for in the first place can you?

So, the expectation of the public for real change when they voted you in has not been realised, and that feels even more depressing. We must stop stripping the public service of its ability to advise governments wisely and truthfully, and resist relying too heavily on private sector consultants to solve public problems, oh and yes – stamp out corruption!

I hate to be the bearer of more bad news, but the democratic impulse is not going anywhere. If people are not happy with your progress they will vote for the other lot. Not necessarily because they think they will do a better job, but to punish you for not meeting their expectations. Rather churlish of us isn't it, but there you have it – democracy in action.

Some dissatisfied souls still believe democracy means 'rule by the people' – in other words, that the decisions that affect them directly should be made by them. By this criterion, we are of course far from democracy. A lot of Hooselanders stubbornly cling to the idea that democracy means that they should get to decide. In their view, democracy is far more than just deciding who will lead us and let other things, like economics, be left to the market.

And you cannot sit back and put the blame on the public service (or me for that matter) if you lose the election, as you have never invested in the creative thinkers in the service or encouraged them to advance innovative thinking on improving people's lives and developing a more effective public service.

According to a Hooseland Clarion survey of nearly 2,500 public servants, we are eager to become innovative public problem solvers. Two out of three respondents were interested in learning more about specific innovation skills. We need a radical re-imagining of the role of the public service.

Hooseland is not alone in this – globally we're at an all-time high when it comes to cynicism about politicians and politics. There's a decline in voter turnout in country after country – in some places, like the USA where fewer than half of the electorate bothers to vote. Even in ex-Soviet countries, people are disillusioned with politics as usual. There is an increasing distance between big political parties and their voters.

Surely there must be more to democracy than this? Mind you, theorists of democracy viewed 'rule by the people' with ambivalence right from the beginning. The dreams of Locke, Mills, and even Rousseau were hampered by the fear of "mob rule and property overthrow".

We didn't really give democracy a chance from the outset – voting was initially limited to those 'men' that owned land. Only they could vote for their representatives who would govern in their stead and remain independent to maintain political stability. In that sense, it was a negative consent – a rather perverse freedom from arbitrary rule rather than a freedom to decide what to do with their lives.

Perhaps it is impossible to have a truly democratic government if you don't have a democratic society – and our corporate-dominated society is actually a form of economic dictatorship.

It is rooted in most Hooselanders work experience to feel like they have no say, that someone else decides, that they're 'managed'. As a result of cash's stranglehold, honest public debate has been suffocated. Outsiders of the economy (let's face it – most of us) remain outsiders of politics largely because of economic factors. But unlike consumerism, democracy is an active process – and it is a messy business, but it is *our* business, and it is time we took it back.

So now as I look back on the previous four years of my adult life I have to ask myself "Is that all there is?" that song has echoes for me in the promise of true democracy and the justice that I sought from 12 years of age when I woke up to the fact that life is not always fair – and began my journey of trying to make sense of democracy with all the "gleaming promise that it never seems quite able to deliver".

Now we will pay the price for handing over the leadership of our lives to the elected representatives and taking a back seat. We delegated our power and I fear that the backlash from voters swinging to the conservative Opposition will be the downfall of Hooseland and I predict dark times ahead for those that value their freedoms.

Yours in service to the public,

Amber Guette (she/her)

Landslide

Dear Minister

Well, that was a resounding slap in the face from the Hooseland voters wasn't it? I knew the writing was on the wall but had not considered that it would be in all caps and 10 feet tall! This morning's headline in the Clarion says it all – LANDSLIDE!

So now it is official – our time together in service of the public has ended, you will go back to being at the other side of the requests for information and being outraged at what is redacted and accuse the government of hiding information, and the rest of us will sigh and continue to try to serve the public, and the more personally motivated will no doubt try to find a way to earn grace and favour with the new lot....

As some wag once said, "There are lots of frustrations in government, but there is nothing as frustrating as being out of government", something you will now have at least four years to consider.

I don't think I have ever been so depressed as I am right now. Will I go back to working in the public service? Of course I will – just like I stayed there for the eight years prior to your Government's election – because someone has to keep the bastards honest!

It's interesting how the post-election loss raises the question of your legacy. You'd think after four years as government, you'd have a *few* accomplishments that could be wheeled out. Journalists agree that a widely accepted list is hard to find, and vagueness abounds as journalists and commentators clutch at minor accomplishments.

Political commentators have called your Government 'uninspiring' since you wasted political opportunity and you have been attacked by the Opposition as the 'troughing' Government.

I've felt like my energy has slowly been drained these past four years. The years of crisis and upheaval globally have been wasted in many ways under this Government. It was a potential period of time to confront deeply ingrained social, cultural, economic, and environmental ills, and shake things up in a comprehensive manner. Bringing about a 'brighter future' that wasn't just soporific election 'polispeak' was the prize up for grabs and *you* wasted that opportunity so shame on you.

Hooselanders have been sleep walking through the last four years, and now we're waking up and blinking into the harsh light of reality. Maybe things had to get this bad for things to change – we are at an ideal time for Hooselanders to rise up, take a hard look at the world we have created, and start something from the grassroots that was meant to be started four years ago by your Government.

The same economic, environmental and social challenges we were facing four years ago still present themselves to us even more urgently, but it is the social challenges that are fundamentally the most significant as they heavily influence the other two.

In order to satisfy the interests of fewer and fewer people, we have constructed a world of privatised, individualised, fragmented and fleeting social bonds, which has resulted in some of the most catastrophic unintended consequences Hooselanders have ever experienced – the Great 'Othering' of Hooseland society – a growing trench not just between the haves and the have-nots, and the progressive and conservative, but also along racial, religious and gender divides as well.

The repercussions of your behaviour will reverberate for years to come. We should have been world leaders in solving these problems – we are a well-liked nation by the vast majority of the planet, and we had the resources if we used them in the right way to really address the root causes of our problems. It is more complex when the enemy comes from within your trusted circle – it creates a deep sense of unease that something fundamental has shifted in the order of things. And that dear Minister is unforgivable.

Yours in service to the public,

Amber Guette

Amber Guette (she/her)

Who's Sorry Now

Dear Minister

This is the last letter I will be sending you as a Minister as that title will be stripped from you tomorrow as the new Government is sworn in. A time one would hope for us all to reflect on where it all went so wrong. The blame here is on all of us – we thought you would 'shake things up' or 'fix the system' or at the very least 'stop corruption' – well the joke was on us and our wee echo chamber after all wasn't it?

Despite the fact that the vast majority of us in the progressive corner were aware of the corrupt cycle of power and wealth that undermined the working class, we did nothing to change it. We all stood by for eight years under the previous government while corporations crushed trade unions, the backbone of the working class.

And then when you got elected, we had the opportunity to unite the working class to take back power from the emerging oligarchy if we had rallied them, they had had enough of them after eight years. The fact is that you took them for granted and turned your back on the working class in order to gain votes from well heeled 'suburban swing voters'.

In addition, you lobbied big corporations for political funding, and once you started taking money from the pockets of the very wealthy and powerful you risked ending up in *their* pockets. And now Hooseland democracy is at risk because we haven't made the structural changes required to strengthen it, this has just weakened democracy for future generations.

The new Government figures such a large victory legitimises their racist, religious, and anti-minorities ideas, and they will not miss the opportunity to attack the hard-won freedoms of Hooselanders.

Hooselanders were barely spared last time around from what could be considered a mandate to pursue an authoritarian agenda by the new Government.

We need to find a way in the public service to show real stewardship of the public good in order to limit the damage such an emboldened government could inflict on them. I have already had a private secretary at CHAOS tell me that the new Ministers diary is filling up fast with leaders of powerful and wealthy conservative churches (even the ones that do not believe in voting for heaven's sake!) And I don't imagine the topic of conversation is going to be how can we end poverty or love thy neighbour....

Yours in service to the public,

Amber Guette

Amber Guette (she/her)

Somebody That I Used to Know

Dear (no longer the) Minister

It was a very weird full circle to cross paths with you this afternoon as you were carrying your personal items out in a cardboard box to the Opposition building at Parliament (not sure you are supposed to take the vase the government was gifted by China with you, so you should probably put that back...).

Kind of bittersweet to think that this will be the last letter I write you. It has certainly been a journey. I have been looking back at the letters I sent you right at the start and the hope and the excitement just jump off the page at me and I feel a little ill at how naive I was back then.

I hope you will remember my words now that you are the Opposition (again) and keep your vitriol for the thinking of the new Government, not public servants that are trying hard to do the right thing. Just as I explained that we need to remain non-partisan (that promiscuous partisanship is just fucked up basically) when you were in government (and I know that kind of annoyed you because you thought I was supposed to be your ally) it should give you comfort to know the same rules go for the next lot.

A bit of advice – perhaps this time try not to be such a lazy opposition? A strong opposition is just as important to democracy as a strong government.

Despite everything (maybe even because of it?) my belief that true public service is a calling, not a job, a sense of where you fit in the world not a career, has not changed. Yes, it is the duty and the privilege of public servants to work with the Government of the day, but first and fore-mostly with the long-term best interest of *all* Hooselanders. As I said earlier – loyalty is for dogs not public servants – any "loyalty" we owe is to the public.

We are the long-term memory of what has come before, and we need to build in the flexibility to seek that which will need to come in the future. As Hooseland Public Servants this should always mean striving towards political neutrality, openness and transparency, free and frank advice and growing our public service based on meritocracy. That you have not diminished, but I know it will continue to be sorely tested by the new Government.

We need to stop taking integrity for granted – no more believing that it is good enough to have implicit integrity and that it is time to build explicit integrity systems that ensure for the public that we are not just *seen* to be doing the right thing but are truly doing so. Doing this is key to our delivering collectively for a better Hooseland in an increasingly fragmented and challenging world.

For your part, take the time in Opposition to reflect on your failures and think about what public service truly means, and whether that is something you can aspire to, if not, please move over and make room for someone that can.

Yours in service to the public (always and forever),

Amber Guette

Amber Guette (she/her)

Dear Reader

I hope you enjoyed the first book of my letters – the battle for Hooseland and the service of the public has only just begun.

If you want to register your interest in being notified when the second tranche of letters is released, then please visit www.DearMinister.net to sign up for a notification. There are also links on there as to where you can hear the songs I shared with the Minister.

You can also email me with your thoughts on what heroic (or not) public service is at Amber.Guette@dearminister.net

Yours in service to the public

Amber Guette (she/her)

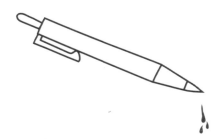

Tired of all her colleagues
whispering in corridors
and crying into their beer
one public servant decided
it was time to talk truth to
power. Perhaps if even just
one Minister (who seemed to
care) was no longer in the
dark things might change
— she just had no idea how
much...

Amber Guette
Publishing Ltd

ISBN 978-0-473-64589-2

9 780473 645892 >